# MAKIA'S BODYGUARD

## JOY BUSSU

Published by Blushing Books
An Imprint of
ABCD Graphics and Design, Inc.
A Virginia Corporation
977 Seminole Trail #233
Charlottesville, VA 22901

Joy Bussu
Makia's Bodyguard

eBook ISBN: 978-1-64563-758-5
Print ISBN: 978-1-64563-759-2
Audio ISBN: 978-1-64563-760-8
v1

Cover Art by ABCD Graphics & Design
This book contains fantasy themes appropriate for mature readers only.
Nothing in this book should be interpreted as Blushing Books' or the author's advocating any non-consensual sexual activity.

## Prologue

Twenty-four-year-old Makia Sallow-Hansen sighed as she crossed the street to the studio she shared with her sister, Sage. Her latest sketches were rolled up in the hard-sided leather sketch bag over her shoulder to protect them from the weather.

Her thigh still stung from the smack of her husband Michael's belt and she was sure he had left a bruise this time. God, she hated him! Waking up knowing he was in that house made her want to vomit. She wanted to leave so bad she could taste it but she knew she couldn't, not yet anyway.

Theirs was a marriage of convenience, no more than a business transaction negotiated by her overbearing and greedy parents and Michael Hansen's lawyers. To this day, the way they bargained and argued about her made her blood boil. The way they referred to her, never by her name, but like she was an object or a piece of land was disgusting!

Makia shook away her bad thoughts and walked into her studio, smiling. Sage was already setting up for her first photo shoot of the day while old school Tupac echoed around the room.

"Sissy! I thought you weren't coming down here until this afternoon," Sage called over her shoulder, moving a lounge chair into the strong beams of her circle of lights.

Makia hated her parents and hell, she hated most of her snotty, stuck up family to be honest with only two exceptions: their paternal grandmother Lola and her big sister Sage. She would do anything for 'the two halves of her heart', as she called them and this was exactly why she was in the situation she was in right now. For Sage and her grandmother to be safe, Makia would gladly walk to Hell and back if she had to and she knew Sage would do the same for her.

"That was the original plan before 'Minute Man' got on my damn nerves this morning. He is such a whiny bitch! I cannot wait until this shit is over, for real," Makia snapped, putting down her stuff and walking over to help Sage move the iron table she wanted in her shot from the corner of the room. The sisters had nicknamed her husband the 'Minute Man' because he was weak as hell in all aspects of life, especially in the bedroom, but his ego wouldn't let him just take the loss so he was known to get physical from time to time, like this morning with the belt.

"I know that weak-stroking bastard didn't put his hands on you again, did he?" Sage stood up, put her hands on her hips, and began scanning Makia for bruises.

Michael was a big man and in most women's eyes he was quite handsome and a catch, especially with all those zeros and commas in his bank account. However Makia was not and never had been impressed by the cars, homes and money he had, not even before she knew what type of man he was.

He was a fucking bully who intimidated people by throwing his weight and money around. However he found out very early in their marriage that even with her 5'4" stature Makia was not intimidated in the least and she could hold her own. No one but Sage knew that when her parents signed them up for ballet when Sage was seven and she was five, Makia snuck into the gym next door and talked her way into boxing lessons instead since the ballet teacher and the boxing instructor were husband and wife and the money went to the same place anyways.

Michael had size but she had the skill and they'd had many a battle in their first two years of marriage. The only reason she continued to put up with it was because of the threats he made against Sage and her grandmother. Because of how quick she was to hit back, he kept his hands to himself for the most part and focused more on sneak attacks.

"Nothing that I couldn't handle, sis, you know how I get down. I do need you to check the back of my thigh though, it's still stinging. Did he break the skin?" Makia lifted up her long skirt and turned her back to Sage. Sage's sudden intake of breath let Makia know it was looking pretty bad back there.

"What the fuck, Makia? What did he hit you with? I swear to God, one day I'm going to kill his bitch ass for this! Why don't you just leave, Kia? Nothing is worth this kind of shit, especially since the only ones benefiting from this fucking marriage is Minute Man and Jason and Evelyn," Sage said, referring to their parents with an eye roll and a grumble. Even when she was the one who mentioned her parents' names, it still set Sage off.

Makia knew Sage didn't care about her parents pulling their financial support or disowning her since finding out about her lifestyle. She could honestly take her last breaths on earth without ever seeing or hearing from them again for all she cared and Makia was right there with her. Sage's biggest concern, though, was Makia and them using their sisterly bond and their grandmother to blackmail Makia into marrying Michael.

The day Makia told Sage that their parents had sold Michael the property that housed their condo and studio, as well as their grandmother's house to secure the marriage, they died as far as the sisters were concerned.

"It was a belt and it's only five more years, Sage or sooner if my lawyer can find a loophole to get me out of this shit. I refuse to let us lose everything we worked so hard to build just because Jason and Evelyn went bankrupt and used me to pad their pockets," Makia answered, closing her eyes against the sudden sting when Sage lightly touched the angry mark on the back of her thigh.

"We would be all right, we could keep the studio and Grandma Lo's house. We have enough in our savings and your trust to do both," Sage mumbled, biting her bottom lip thoughtfully. She had grabbed the first aid kit and was tending to Makia's thigh as they talked.

"How Sage? This is our life's dream and you and I know Michael would have this place bulldozed to the ground the minute I left. Grandma Lo's house too! And apparently the terms of my trust have been changed and tied into this sham of a marriage, so I can't collect until I have my first child. For now he owns the properties and because of that, he owns me for five more years. You and I both know even if we took the money we've saved to relocate, he would just buy that property too. We can outwit the idiot but we can't out money him, sissy," Makia reasoned sadly, looking down into Sage's angry scowl over her shoulder as she secured the bandage on the back of her thigh.

"I can't watch this happen for five more years Kia, I can't! I am willing to lose everything before I allow you to endure this any longer, it's sick! And I will find a way to wreck all of their shit before I ever allow you to have that barracuda's baby! Jason and Evelyn can go to hell! Fuck them and that trust fund!" Sage spat, putting everything back in the first aid kit and walking back across the studio to put it away.

"I know you would, Sage but I'm not willing to let you do

that, also I'm not having a baby so don't trip. They took everything away from you, you even had to drop out of school because of them. They are not taking away our studio or Grandma's home, not while I'm still breathing. I can handle Michael and I can handle our parents if they resurface again, okay? Just continue to shine so I can throw your success in their faces!"

Makia hugged her sister before picking up her stuff and heading to the second floor of the studio where her things were. She heard Sage's first client of the day arrive and soon the repetitive click of her cameras brought Makia enough peace and calm to start painting.

Despite the rough start of her morning, the subject's face that stared up at her from her unrolled canvas caused her to smile. The subject of her sketch was every woman's fantasy personified, tall and handsome with a muscular build, but it was his hair that he wore in long, perfectly maintained dreads that took her under.

Most of the time they were either braided into a style or ponytail so the first time she had the pleasure of seeing him with his crowning glory hanging over his shoulders wild and free on full display was the day she stopped fighting with herself and admitted her attraction to him. That day he became not only her one and only heart's desire, but also the accelerant that was going to burn her parents and Michael Hansen's money grabbing dreams to the ground and allow her and Sage to rise from the ashes.

## Chapter 1

*Four years ago*

"Y ou know Sage won't agree to this without a fight," Makia overheard her father Jason Sallow whisper to her mother Evelyn. They were talking in his office on the first floor of their mansion with the door half-closed. Makia stopped in her tracks at the sound of her sister's name and crept closer to eavesdrop.

"So fucking what? Let her fight as long as she does it. She has no choice; she owes us, Jason!" her mother snapped. Makia could see her pacing back and forth clutching a highball glass from her vantage point. Her eyes moved from her mother to her father. His normal well-kept appearance was gone: his hair was all over his head from him running his hands through it in frustration, he wasn't wearing a tie, his cufflinks were gone, and his sleeves were rolled up.

"But Michael Hansen, Evelyn? I know for a fact he's not a good guy. People talk, Evelyn, there has to be someone else," her father reasoned trying to take her mother into his arms.

She pushed him away and threw back the rest of her drink before going over to his wet bar for a refill.

Makia deduced whatever was going on was really bad, her mother never drank and now that she thought about it, her father was home way too early from work.

"We are out of time, Jason, the money is gone! It's too late to find someone else and besides, no one is offering the amount he is. Sage is marrying Michael Hansen and that's final! I don't care what she says! Now get on board so we can move forward on this!" her mother whispered loudly, throwing back her second drink and slamming the glass down on his desk.

Makia barely made it to the maid's closet to hide before her mother stormed out of his office and up the stairs to her bedroom. A few minutes after hearing the door slam, Makia snuck out of the maid's closet and out of the house to go find Sage. She was just about to jump in her car to drive to their studio when her father appeared and came walking towards her, still looking a little worse for wear.

"Makia, just getting home? Don't make any plans for the evening and if you have some cancel them, we are having a special guest for dinner," her father demanded, rushing by her and climbing in his custom-made Ferrari and roaring down the driveway.

Makia glared after him before getting into her midnight blue mustang. She quickly googled the name Michael Hansen and her stomach churned with fear for her sister and disgust for her greedy ass parents. This was who they were trying to marry her sister off to? So what his net worth was 9.6 billion dollars, he was 45 fucking years old, Sage was 22!

She almost wondered how the hell people as selfish as Jason and Evelyn Sallow managed to have her and her sister before she looked up at the picture of her grandmother Lola, her, and Sage from last Mother's day hanging from her rearview mirror and remembered how her grandma had practically raised the two while their parents attended business meetings and charity banquets. Every good part of them was owed to their grandmother.

Just when she was about to back out of the driveway, her mother came charging down the front steps and over to her car. "Makia! Thank God you're home! There is a lot to do, we are having a couple of special guests over for dinner and I need your help." Her mom opened her car door and practically snatched her out of her car. "Hurry, go put your stuff away and go help Sarah and Brin set up the formal dining room, then come and find me when you're done." Before Makia could say anything, her mother was already rushing back up the steps into the house.

"Fuck!" Makia groaned, throwing her head back and pulling her phone out of the back pocket of her shorts as she walked up to the house. Why did she have to be there for dinner? She quickly shot off a message to Sage telling her not to come home, to stay the night at Joslyn's and that she would explain later.

She had just locked her screen when her mom came back outside and snatched her iPhone from her hands. "Makia, did you not hear what I said? We have guests coming for dinner! No distractions, I'll give you your phone back later!" her mom snapped and rushed back up the stairs but waited for Makia to go inside with her.

Makia felt the tip of her ears burning in frustration, she was twenty fucking years old and her mom just took her phone like she was twelve! She couldn't wait until all of her and Sage's plans were in place so they could move the fuck away from here for good!

"Makia!" came from the opposite end of the house in Evelyn's nasally voice, three hours later.

Makia rushed out of her room pushing her last earring in place. While she had six piercing in her ears, three on each side, she decided to play nice and wear matching gold hoops that got smaller from top to bottom instead of the mix-and-match she usually did. Her hair was down and she had decorated herself with minimal makeup, black jeans, a dark blue short sleeved silk blouse and black suede ballet slippers. She saw no need to dress up because she saw no need for her to even be at the table. This dinner was a fucking joke.

She and Sage were both very beautiful women; they could pass for twins even though they were two years apart with their mixed heritage stemming from their Italian mother and African American father. Both were born nearly white but their skin darkened to a cinnamon brown hue by the time they were one year old. The sisters had always turned heads with their heart shaped faces with dark brown eyes and semi full lips. They were also curvy like their grandmother Lola and wore their hair long in its naturally curly state. Both were relatively short, with Sage standing just barely an inch over Makia.

"What? I'm right here, why are you yelling like that?" she asked, descending the stairs, already annoyed.

Her mother was pacing back and forth again, dressed to kill but clutching a glass looking like she could shatter it if she were anymore worked up. "Where is Sage? Where the hell is your sister?" she demanded as soon as Makia hit the landing.

Makia fought the urge to smirk knowingly at her mother, thank God her sister had listened and stayed away! "I don't know, you took my phone, remember?" With a shrug, Makia tossed her curly hair over her shoulder and turned to walk to the dining room.

Her mother snatched her by the arm and turned her back to face her while digging her long fingernails into Makia's arm.

"If you have any idea where she might be you better tell me! She's about to ruin everything!" Her mother yelled in her face, shaking her to emphasize the urgency of the situation. Her mother's eyes were shiny and glazed from the brandy she was drinking like water.

Makia pushed her mother's hands off of her and backed away from her, looking at her like she was crazy, "Mom! Calm down! Like I said, I have no idea where she is or where she might even be because *you took my phone*! Now, before these special guests of yours get here, might I strongly suggest you get it together? Sheesh!" Makia pivoted and stalked out of the foyer and towards the dining room.

She ran right into her father who looked equally stressed. "Makia, where is–"

Makia stopped him mid-sentence, already pissed off. "Dad, like I just told Mom I don't know where Sage is, okay? Mom took my phone and has yet to return it so I guess dinner is going to have to happen without her. Now if you will please excuse me, I have to go find a sweater or shrug to pull on to cover the bruises Mom just left on my arm before your guests get here!" Makia stomped off to the mud room in search of her favorite white sweater, where Sarah would put it after doing laundry.

Their cook Mattie rang the bell to announce the start of dinner just as she pushed her arms through the sleeves of her sweater. She was still annoyed with her parents but happy as hell Sage was nowhere to be found and smart enough not to answer their parents phone calls.

Humming to herself, Makia walked into the dining room and settled down in the chair closest to the door for a quick exit once dessert was served. She smiled at a servant named Brin as she poured Makia's sparkling water into her glass. "Sage said to tell you to meet her at the studio when all of this is over so you can tell her what's going on." Growing up, if she and Sage weren't with their grandmother they were with the servants and Sarah, Brin and Mattie were woven into all her childhood memories.

Her parents and their guests still weren't at the table yet, likely because they were in her father's office so they could explain why Sage wasn't joining them for dinner before they sat down to eat. Minutes later, her father led her mother to her seat with a somber look on his face. Michael Hansen came next, whose face Makia remembered from her Google search, followed by another man she could only describe as remarkably beautiful.

Handsome was just not enough to describe him. He was beautiful, like a living work of art. Nothing about him seemed real, his smooth light brown skin wrapped around his muscular frame like shrink wrap. He stood about 5'11" tall, with hypnotizing light brown bedroom eyes framed in long eyelashes and an almost innocent but seductive smile.

She instantly loved everything about him, especially the way his mustache hugged his full, soft looking lips and how he looked like he had a five o' clock shadow of a beard. Her fingers tingled with the urge to grab a charcoal pencil and sketch pad to capture his likeness. In that moment she felt like he could be her muse for the next 100 years.

"Makia, I want you to meet two of my business associates, Michael Hansen and his business partner, Hayes Purcell. They're looking to acquire some of the assets my company is liquidating," her father introduced with an uncomfortable smile and a nervous glance at her mother.

Makia bit the inside of her cheek in anger at her sister being referred to as a 'liquidated asset' but plastered a fake smile on her face and extended her hand to them both. Michael's hand was sweaty and slimy and she hated the vomit-inducing way he looked down at her as he brought her hand to his mouth to kiss. His lips barely made contact with her hand when she snatched her hand away and turned to shake hands with Hayes.

Ignoring the immediate jolt of attraction that shot through her, she reminded herself he was part of the enemy camp and pulled her hand away from his grasp too. His eyes lingered on her face before pulling the napkin from his plate and placing it in his lap.

"Nice to meet you both," she mumbled before turning and moving back to her seat at the table.

"I hope you both like seafood, I had Mattie make her world-famous lobster bisque and crab cakes for dinner. For dessert, we'll have 7-Up cake and key lime pie. I have opted to forgo the salad this evening and start with the bisque," Makia's mother announced with a plastic smile.

"As I was explaining to Mr. Hansen, your sister had a last-minute opportunity she just couldn't miss, right, Makia?" her father asked her nervously with a plastic smile of his own.

Makia picked up her soup spoon and sighed as Sarah placed a bread bowl of bisque in front of her before looking at all four of them sitting at the table. With a shrug, she said, "I honestly have no idea. If that's where you say Sage is, Dad, then I guess that's where she is! I haven't talked to her since this morning." She narrowed her eyes at her mother. Hell yeah, she was still salty about her phone!

"Please forgive Makia, she told me she wasn't feeling well earlier and we insisted she still join us for dinner. I guess she still isn't feeling one hundred percent yet," her mom simpered at Michael and Hayes before giving Makia a hard look, her face tinged with embarrassment.

Makia rolled her eyes at her mother and took a drink out of her water glass. She didn't care if she was being rude, she didn't know these men nor did she want to, especially knowing the only reason why they were here was so they could basically barter Sage off to Michael. As soon as dessert was served, she was leaving and spending the night at the studio. Her parents were tripping.

"So, your parents have told me all about Sage and her photography. What is it that you do, Makia?" Michael asked her while eating his soup. Every time he paused he would look over at her, she could feel his gaze raking up and down her body.

"I'm an artist," she answered shortly, returning to her soup. The look her mother gave her almost made her laugh, her face appearing seconds from exploding in anger. Like she cared! Why was she even here?

"Well, that doesn't tell me shit, girl, tell me what you do," Michael asked a little too loudly and chuckled, pushing his empty soup bowl forward before sitting back in his chair, smiling.

Pushing her own bowl away she noticed some things, his smile didn't meet his eyes his brows were furrowed, and how Hayes was glaring at Michael who was waiting impatiently for an answer.

"I paint, draw, sculpt. I do it all, like I said I am an artist. I'm studying art at George Mason University for the time being but I'm kicking around the idea of maybe transferring to Pratt or Venice next year to complete my studies," Makia answered, trying to remain calm by finishing off her glass of water afterwards.

"Hmm, interesting and what will you be able to do with a degree in *art?*" Michael asked, smirking at her and shaking his head like she was a joke to him.

"Whatever I choose to, Mr. Hansen. You see, unlike you, Mr. Purcell, and my parents here, my passions are not driven by the all-mighty dollar." She thanked Brin for refilling her water glass and refused her main course. "Don't get me wrong, I like money just as much as the next person, just look at how comfortably I am able to live because of it, but I'm not willing to sell my soul for it." She glared over at her parents as she pushed her chair back and stood up from the table.

"Now, as nice as this conversation and dinner has been, I believe it's past time I excuse myself. That illness my mother spoke of earlier has suddenly come back in full force and right now I am suddenly fighting the urge to puke," Makia snapped, tossing her napkin on the table and leaving the dining room.

She heard rapid footsteps behind her and stopped walking. She turned around quickly ready to have an argument with her mother, but to her surprise, it was Mattie.

"Here, I don't want you leaving the house without it. She is so fit to be tied right now because Sage no showed for dinner that she won't even notice we snuck it out of her room. Now hurry up and go before she comes looking for you," Mattie said, handing Makia her phone and hugging her quickly before rushing back to the kitchen.

---

Makia must have broken every speed limit from Princess Anne Hills to their studio a mile past Virginia Beach. She felt like bugs were crawling on her skin, remembering how gross and nasty everything about Michael Hansen felt. Her grandmother was right, old men really do give you worms!

She parked two blocks over in the art supply store's parking lot and took the back entrance to their studio, just in case one of her parents did a drive-by past the studio looking for her or Sage. She didn't see Sage's car so she assumed she left her car at Joslyn's and had Joslyn drop her off.

"Sage? Sage are you still here?" Makia called out, coming up the backstairs.

"Oh, thank God! Kia, what the hell is going on?" Sage rushed over to her, hugging her close for a few seconds.

Tears she didn't even realize she was holding back spilled

from Makia's eyes. Sage helped her sit down and grabbed a bottle of water from their kitchenette. "Sage, Mom and Dad are tripping, like really tripping! They've lost their fucking minds!" Makia cried, trying to catch her breath.

"Okay, Sissy, I need you to calm down and just tell me what's going on." Sage sat next to her, taking her hands in her own.

After Makia drank half of the bottle of water she felt calm enough to talk. "I overheard Dad and Mom talking about you when I got home from my classes this afternoon. They didn't know I was there and Mom was drinking, Sage. I mean like hardcore drinking and Dad looked crazy and stressed. I heard her say you owed them and you had to marry this Michael Hansen guy they were bringing to dinner because the money was gone!" Makia told Sage before she started crying again.

"What? No way, Kia, you had to have heard wrong. Our parents are assholes but they're not 'marry my daughter off to the highest bidder' assholes!" Sage said, actually trying to convince herself even more than Makia. She could hear her heartbeat pounding loudly in her ears.

"Oh, really? Then tell me why I stormed out of dinner with this Michael Hansen prick and his business partner after Mom and Dad kept trying to get me to lie about where you were tonight? I know they've both been blowing your phone up too, huh?" Makia argued, getting heated with her sister for taking things so lightly.

"Still Makia, that doesn't mean they wanted me there to marry the dude, just for me to meet him probably," Sage insisted, biting a small piece of loose skin on her bottom lip nervously.

Makia finished her water and stomped across the room to throw her bottle away. "Yeah, okay, and how many dinners have Mom and Dad insisted this strongly that we attend to meet his business partners? Not one, Sage! He called you a fucking asset he was going to liquidate!"

Sage covered her mouth to keep from screaming. She had always known her parents were relentlessly money driven but even they wouldn't stoop this low, would they?

"Sage, Michael Hansen is worth 9.6 billion dollars. Just let that sink in for a minute. Mom and Dad could pretty much name their damn price and he will gladly pay it for you. I heard Dad say he wanted to find someone else but Mom said there was no time and it had to be him because he could afford it. I heard her say no matter how much you fight this, in the end you are marrying Michael Hansen." Makia grabbed Sage by the shoulders to make her look at her and see that she was serious.

"I just can't believe they would do something like this! I'm not marrying someone I don't know! I would rather die!" Sage screamed and stormed off to go get her own bottle of water. She stood there seething in anger and disbelief when she heard Makia sigh sadly, looking down at her phone.

"Looks like you don't have to, I have a date with Michael Hansen on Thursday. If I don't go they are pulling their monetary support, if I do go they will pay for me to study in Venice next year." Makia held up her phone so Sage could see the message from their mother as tears began to roll down her face again.

## Chapter 2

*Two years ago*

"Seven years Makia, that's all! Seven years and one kid and you can divorce him and everything you acquired in the marriage is yours, free and clear," Evelyn reasoned with Makia on her wedding day.

Makia looked every bit the image of a blushing bride but inside, Makia was ready to set the venue on fire and kill them all. She had pulled every trick in the book she could think of to stall this day while she, her grandmother and Sage scrambled to find her a way out of it.

First she argued she needed to finish her degree, so she spent the last year in Venice attending the art school of her dreams on her parents' dime, then she was able to postpone another nine months for her art show in New York. Of course, she had a bodyguard following her around everywhere she went who also reported to Michael three times a day.

A lonely tear ran down her face as she remembered the day her parents and Michael demanded she return to Virginia and painted her into a corner.

"Makia, I brought you here to tell you, sweetheart, our wedding will be taking place six months from today or you leave me no choice." Michael shook his head in mock sadness as he looked over at her with a predatory glare.

"No choice in what? Mom? Dad? What is he talking about?" she cautiously asked, getting annoyed and tired of all of this. She had her degree, she was making a name for herself in the art world and she and Sage had enough in their savings to survive and run the studio. What the hell could they possibly do to her?

"Well let's just say your parents have sweetened the pot on this deal to ensure my happiness despite all of your stall tactics to delay the wedding." He pushed a stack of papers in front of her and Makia realized in complete disgust and horror that her parents had sold this bastard not only her and Sage's studio but their grandmother's house too!

"Now I strongly suggest you get to planning our dream wedding before I bulldoze you and your dyke sister's studio and sell dear old granny's house and put her in a nursing home where she belongs," Michael snapped, snatching the papers off the table and standing to leave.

Makia glared up at him, knowing the reason why he was so bitter with Sage was that he had all but convinced their parents to marry Sage off, too! He had an associate of his he was trying to merge companies with who, like Michael, wanted to boost his image so he offered up Sage and talked their parents into it, but before they could even approach Sage to tell her about the arrangement, Sage had finally worked up the courage to come out to her parents and move in with Joslyn.

Needless to say, all hell broke loose, and her parents immediately disowned her. With no marriage, Michael's deal fell through and he'd had Sage in his crosshairs ever since for costing him money. This all happened when Makia was still in Venice and the only reason they still had the studio was because they held it over Makia's head to keep her line.

She knew her parents were desperate for money but what the fuck? Her hypocrite of a father was willing to sell his mom out again? She was floored!

They all watched Michael leave her father's office.

"The minute this bullshit ass wedding is over, I never want to see or hear from either one of you again. You are dead to me."

---

Now here she sat, six months later, thinking about arson and murder because her day of reckoning had finally come. Makia sat still while the makeup artist repaired the streak her tear had made. She glared at her mother silently as she ran over the highlighted parts of the contract regarding her marriage to Michael Hansen as well as her prenup. She made sure to focus on those items or specific words they missed, as those were her safety net, her passport to freedom and she would use all of them to get her out of this shit when the time was right. She just had to make sure her grandmother and Sage would be okay, too.

She was good at playing the role of a loser conceding to their win, little did they know she counted the days when she would be able to destroy them all.

---

## Present day

"Makia, now I told you I needed you dressed and ready to go by six. What the hell is the hold up?" Michael asked her storming into her suite of rooms.

Makia was standing in her closet holding a plum colored jumpsuit in her hands. She had already showered after coming from the studio and her hair and makeup were already done.

"Michael, it's five. You said be ready at six and I will be ready at six. I've never been late before so why would today be the first day? Now can you please leave so I can finish getting dressed?" she asked trying her best to keep her attitude in check.

He frowned at the bandage Sage had put on her leg. "What is that, what happened to your leg?" he asked with a frown, like he didn't know.

Makia didn't even bother to answer, she just glared at him with an arched eyebrow and parked her hand on her hip. She watched him open and close his fists before his jaw jumped in anger and he quickly moved towards her. Hanging her jumpsuit back in her closet, she turned quickly and continued to glare at him.

"Clock's ticking, Michael. We can either get to this investor's dinner on time or get into some real shit, your choice," Makia snapped, waiting for him to make a move.

She watched his nostrils flare like a bull as he backed away from her like she was going to attack him from behind or something knowing good and damn well he had nothing to worry about. That was his MO not hers! For the most part, she left him alone as long as he left her alone.

"You're getting real slick at the mouth, Makia, and I'm getting real tired of it," he mumbled, walking out of her suite.

"Like I fucking care," Makia mumbled and rolled her eyes, grabbing her jumpsuit again and got dressed as quickly as her shaking hands would allow her to. She said a silent prayer that Hayes was truly a man of his word and her days in this hell-hole were numbered.

---

### One and half years ago

"Good morning, Mrs. Hansen. It's been awhile, how are you?" The receptionist at the main desk asked, smiling at her when she walked into Michael's office for the second time in her life. The first was for a bullshit engagement lunch the partners threw for them. Now he interrupted her day and summoned her there to meet him for lunch for some damn reason and she was pissed about it. She had to reschedule the class she was teaching at the learning annex near her studio.

Her hand was swollen and bruised from trying to take Michael's head off for trying to backhand her when she questioned him about their new cook, so the last place she wanted to be was anywhere his stupid ass was!

He was outside of his rabid ass mind if he thought he was going to trap her in a seven-year marriage and abuse her too! You would have thought he had learned his lesson on their honeymoon when he slept in another room because after he hit her, she went to war on his ass! They even took separate flights back home afterward.

"Please call me Makia and I'm fine. How about you, Gayle?" Makia asked, returning her smile.

"I'm doing well, you remembered my name! Thank you for that, most don't even bother to try." Gayle pressed the button to open the huge glass doors that lead to the executive offices and waved, still smiling as she went back to answering the phones.

Makia sighed, knowing Gayle was referring to Michael and

walked through the doors before making her way down the long hall of offices to Michael's. She was reaching for the door to have his assistant inform him that she was there when someone tapped her lightly on the shoulder.

She turned and found herself looking into the hypnotic light brown eyes of Michael's business partner, Hayes Purcell. Makia had made it a point to avoid him at all costs after her wedding as she always felt what she called a 'desire to draw him' in full force when he was near. She was never around when he stopped by the house and since she never came to their office, she hadn't seen him in over a year, and yet that tingling feeling was inching up her spine even as her mind screamed warnings at her.

"I heard you might be stopping by today and wanted to make sure to talk to you. Nice to see you again, Makia. Some of the partners and I were beginning to think maybe Michael locked you away in an ivory tower or something," Hayes remarked, extending his hand for her to shake.

The same jolt she felt the first time she met him, ricocheted through her now. She quickly pulled her hand away and read-justed the bandage wrapped around her hand, mainly her bruised knuckles. Now she knew why 'Minute Man' had called her in to show her off.

"I'm sorry, I didn't notice you were hurt! I didn't make it worse, did I?" he asked with a frown of concern on his face when he looked from her injured hand and back again.

The door behind them opened and Michael stepped out in the hallway. "Hey babe. Gayle buzzed Michelle and told her you were here and on your way to my office. I was beginning to think you got lost or something," Michael informed her, stepped up, and put his arm possessively around her waist with a smug smile she knew was directed at Hayes.

"Well, Hayes stopped me to say hello and I figured it would

be considered rude not to say it back," Makia explained, forcing a smile in Michael's direction.

"Yeah, I was telling her we have been giving you a hard time about not seeing her around here, I was just making sure I didn't hurt her hand when you stepped out." Hayes' eyes dropped back down to the bandaged hand in question.

"I keep telling Makia she goes too hard in her kickboxing class," Michael blushed and chuckled nervously, looking down at her. If looks could kill, he would be six feet under.

Makia shifted her thoughts and fought the urge to roll her eyes so hard it made them start watering. "And as I have told him several times before, it's not the class that caused the injury, but the big, old, heavy bag we have hanging at the house." She could barely muster even a fake smile in his direction this time before moving out of Michael's grip. When she looked over at Hayes again, she could tell by the small smirk on his face he had noticed her dig and her sidestep, not that she cared.

"Interesting, I didn't know you kickboxed, Makia. I know of a gym over on 4th that's pretty lit if you ever want a change of scenery," Hayes offered, while reaching behind him and opening his office door.

"Hmm, something to consider, my studio is near 4th. I am always up for a new challenge to add to my home workouts, right babe?" Makia asked with a sadistic smile in Michael's direction and extra sarcasm on the 'babe' before taking notice of the fact that Hayes was suppressing a laugh. She started to slowly move back down the hall towards the glass doors that led to the lobby and elevators.

"Well, it was nice to see you again, Makia. Take care of that hand," Hayes called out, leaning on the doorframe of his office with his hands in his pockets.

It pissed her off that she once again noticed how attractive he was considering who he was to Michael. That alone should have kept her disgust at an all-time high! She caught his gaze slowly moving up her frame before he turned and walked inside his office closing the door behind him.

Michael cleared his throat and Makia stopped walking and looked over her shoulder at him. He was still in the same spot in front of Hayes' office.

"Coming, honey? You said you made reservations for 2:30, it's already 1:50 and I know how much you hate to arrive anywhere late," she asked sickeningly sweetly before moving further down the hall and towards the exit. There was no way in hell she was being paraded around his office like his fucking trophy, she did that enough at the stuffy dinner parties he was always dragging her to.

---

"Makia! What's up, girl?" Someone called out as she worked the heavy bag a month later. She was bathed in sweat, having just finished a kickboxing class, and stayed behind to work the bag some because she was still pissed.

She paused her music, pulled one earbud out and stopped the bag from swinging as Hayes walked over to the corner where she was. When she was in this type of headspace, she made it a point to distance herself from other people. She was a grunter when she got worked up.

"Oh. Hi, Hayes," she said, grabbing her towel and pressing it to her forehead, being less than friendly. Noticing how good he looked in his t-shirt and gym shorts added fuel to her already burning rage. Right now anyone who had anything to do with Michael's bitch ass was in her crosshairs.

"Oh thanks for asking, I'm good, great actually, business is good, so life is good. I see you finally took my advice and came to check this place out," Hayes sarcastically stated, reaching up to grab the chains of the punching bag she was working on to make it stop swinging.

Makia's eyes narrowed at him. Couldn't he tell she was in no mood for conversation? She wanted to be rude and wanted to go back to punching the bag but she knew she would never hear the end of it from Michael and it just wasn't worth the fight. "Yeah, thanks again, that class was brutal but I loved it. This place is a lot closer to my studio than my regular gym is too."

She took a drink of water from her water bottle, grabbed a pair of focus mitts near the wall, and brought them back to him. Since he wanted to talk and mess up her concentration, might as well make his ass useful.

"After that class, you still ain't done? Damn girl, I see you," Hayes said, shaking his head impressed, slipping the mitts on.

She waited patiently while he got his stance right and held up his hands, all she could see was Michael's bullying ass stepping into the studio interrupting Sage's photo shoot with some bullshit.

*"What's up, Sage, where's the wifey at?" Michael asked loudly, turning off Sage's music as he walked in.*

*Makia quickly threw her paintbrush into its water cup and stormed down the stairs, hearing Sage's voice echo as she apologized profusely to her client.*

*"Michael, what the fuck?" Makia rushed over to him, whispering fiercely. Rage was too weak of a description to begin to describe what she was feeling at that moment. She grabbed him by the sleeve and dragged him through the back out of the studio.*

*"I haven't been able to reach you for over five hours, Makia, and since you continue to refuse my bodyguard suggestion, I had to make sure you were okay." He gave her a smug smile as he reached out to push a curl out of her face.*

*She slapped his hand away glaring at him. "Don't touch me, you fucking psycho! You burned my fucking shoes this morning, all of them and you really expect me to answer your phone calls and texts? Man, fuck you!"*

*"See? That attitude right there is exactly why I had to do a pop-up*

visit. I will not be ignored, Makia." He grabbed her to him and she drove her foot down hard on the top of his foot.

"And I told you not to touch me!" Makia snapped, glowering at him. She was silently daring him to try to do something to her out here in public.

"Fuck is wrong with you? Don't you know I have the power to shut all this shit down right now? Until the seven years are up, I, me, Michael fucking Hansen, owns this shit right here! I told you not to fucking try to play me, Makia!" He shouted loudly enough to cause passersby to stare, pointing back at the studio.

"And I told you not to fucking play me, Michael! I'm here in this bull-shit ass marriage, I told you and my money hungry ass parents I will give you seven years, I will play the role of doting wife in public, boost your ego and image or what the fuck ever I'm here for, but I will not let you destroy what me and Sage have built in that time! In your haste to prove a point today, did you forget Sage has a restraining order on you from threatening her the last time? Wonder what your colleagues would have to say if they saw you on the 5 o'clock news being led away in handcuffs for violating it?" Makia threatened tapping her finger to her cheek, smiling evilly when he balked.

"You are such a scheming bitch sometimes," he spat with the realization she was right.

"I might be but I guarantee you this, Michael, I will never be a dumb ass one. Now the only thing that's keeping you out of handcuffs right now is me, so I strongly suggest you take your bullying ass back in there and pay Sage for her time and a little extra for the lost revenue you caused her and apologize to her client if he is still in there before I give my sister the go ahead to make a phone call." Makia stared him in the eyes with all the hostility she felt towards him.

After several minutes, he backed down and moved towards the back door of the studio.

"Oh, and Michael? That restraining order includes phone calls too." Her evil smile spread even wider across her face as she saw him ball up his fists and release them angrily before going to apologize to Sage. Makia was right on his heels to make sure he did exactly what she told him to do.

That same smile resurfaced now as she started swinging, taking all of her frustration out on Hayes and the focus mitts. Haye's eyes widened in surprise before he repositioned his stance to keep his balance and absorb her continuous blows. The look of alarm in his face made her smile wider and swing harder. Every feeling of frustration she felt in the last three years went into her jabs. The smug look on Michael's face when he got something else to hold over her head as leverage, his overbearing personality, hell, everything about the marriage!

Every day she was with Michael, she felt more and more of the caring and compassionate woman she was, slipping away. She was becoming cold and calculated, driven by anger. Her life had turned into a never-ending game of chess that she was hell bent on winning and she hated it.

She hated Michael but she hated her parents more for putting them all in this situation! Fuck them! Fuck Michael! Fuck this marriage, she just wanted her life back!

Tears of hatred, frustration, and pain began to pour from her eyes as her muscles screamed out in pain for her to stop swinging. She continued to throw jabs at Hayes nonstop, the burning in her shoulders and arms, the throbbing in her knuckles, even the ache in her thighs and calves just incentivized her. She didn't want to stop, she couldn't stop, she had to keep swinging. She had to protect herself and those she loved from Michael's sadistic ass and the only way to do that was to keep swinging, swinging and swinging!

"Whoa, whoa, whoa! Makia, chill! Makia, it's me, Hayes. Makia listen to my voice. Listen to me, honey," Hayes said dropping his voice and the focus mitts while dodging her fists until he was able to catch them both in his big hands to stop her from throwing more fury-filled punches.

Sweat and tears poured down Makia's face, blurring her vision. Her chest rose and fell as she tried to catch her breath and understand what happened. The moment clarity hit she dissolved into a sobbing mess.

"Hey, what's that all about?" Hayes asked softly, pulling her into his arms and rocking her while she cried.

When it was obvious she wasn't going to stop anytime soon, he scooped her into his arms, carried her into an office near the locker room, and sat on the couch, holding her while she cried.

Makia's swollen eyes fluttered open. Her body's rocking sobs were now soft hiccups as she sat up and realized where she was and who she was with. She scrambled off his lap and moved to the door to leave.

"Makia, Makia, chill. What's going on? Seriously, tell me what's wrong," he pleaded, holding the office door closed to prevent her from leaving and watching her with concern.

Fear moved through her. Not only did she finally break down but she did it in front of Michael's business partner? Just fucking great, this was the last thing she needed.

"Nah, I'm good, sorry about that. I didn't mess up your shirt, did I?" Makia asked, trying again to leave.

Hayes held the door closed. "It's all good, now talk to me, Makia. What the hell was that all about? You've obviously been holding some shit in for a while," he answered in a quiet stern voice without bothering to take his eyes off of her to check his shirt.

"Nothing, I get really wrapped up in my workouts sometimes. Like I said, I'm sorry but I'm fine," she insisted, praying to God whoever's office this was wasn't coming back before she could get out of it. The last thing she needed was for something like this to get back to Michael, especially when she was still winning the war of the bodyguard and battle of keeping him away from Sage and their studio. All hell would break loose.

Hayes sighed in frustration. "Makia, you and I both know

you are not okay. Tell me what's wrong. You're not going anywhere until you do," he stated, taking a chance he could reach her and reassure her she was safe with him.

She was about to panic when her eyes landed on a picture of Hayes and a large dog on the desk. Makia bit the inside of her cheek thoughtfully as her eyes narrowed suspiciously at Hayes.

"Is this your office, Hayes?" she asked with an undertone of attitude.

He looked around the office and nodded before looking back down at her. "Yeah, this is my office. I own this place." He shrugged like it didn't matter.

"Wow, he will stop at nothing to keep me in check. Unbelievable," Makia muttered, glaring up at Hayes accusingly.

"Huh? What the hell are you talking about, Makia?" he asked, giving her a confused look.

"So you're going to sit here and try to tell me you inviting me to the boxing class at this gym, the gym you own, has nothing to do with Michael?" Makia asked with a smirk, putting her hand on her hip, still fearful but getting angry and anger trumped fear's ass any day!

Hayes still had his hand resting on the door to keep Makia inside as he frowned down at her, getting heated at what she was accusing him of.

"That is exactly what I'm telling you, Makia. When Michael mentioned you took kickboxing classes I thought you might like the ones here. You're bleeding, mind if I patch you up before you storm out of here?" he asked, gazing down at her hands before grabbing one and showing her what he was talking about.

She blinked in surprise at her body's even stronger reaction to his touch this time, tingles ran up her spine giving her a chill before traveling around her body and centralizing between her legs. *Um no!* Her voice of reason screamed loudly in her ears.

When she didn't fight him on it, he walked her over to the couch and sat her down as she watched him reach for a first aid kit from the shelf next to the couch. Sitting next to her, he pulled off her gloves carefully and unwrapped both of her hands. In her fit of rage, she managed to bust her knuckles on both hands and they were black and blue and swollen with blood staining the tops of her hands.

Hayes whistled through his teeth slowly, looking at her injuries. "Damn girl, you did some damage. I could feel the heat behind your jabs. It felt like you were trying to take somebody's head off."

"Nah never that, I'm just a passionate person. I'm an artist so I train just as hard as I work," she answered dismissively before wincing when he pressed the cotton ball of antiseptic to her knuckles.

Hayes grabbed another cotton ball to start the process all over again and shook his head, looking at Makia. "Makia, I'm not blind nor am I stupid, so don't try coming at me like I am. Something is wrong and I wish to God you would trust me and let me help you." Hayes continued to work on her hands so he missed her rolling her eyes at him.

"Funny that you, of all people, would expect me to trust you," Makia snapped and tried to stay still when he sprayed antibacterial spray on her knuckles that burned so bad it made her eyes water.

Hayes shook his head and ignored her remark. This was the second time she alluded to him being shady and her thinking of him that way was really bugging him, especially when it wasn't true. He took his time and carefully wrapped her hands before lifting her chin to make eye contact.

"Now that that's done, wanna tell me what I did that got you feeling some type of way about me?"

Makia moved her head so he wasn't touching her anymore, him holding her hands while he cleaned her cuts already had her ready to lean into him for comfort. What the hell was wrong with her? He was the enemy! Wasn't he?

"You going to answer me, baby girl, or leave me hanging, glaring at me with those pretty eyes of yours?" Hayes asked, flashing a smile that knocked her entire world off its axis.

She didn't know what the hell was going on with her but she did know she needed to leave this office. The fact he had the nerve to sit there like he didn't know what the hell Michael and her parents did, like he wasn't sitting right there in her fucking dining room!

That thought was like cold water in the face. She opened her mouth but closed it before a syllable came out. She was kind of afraid of the blow back, especially knowing how messed up her hands were, they were her tools after all. Then she thought *fuck it!* If she was going to have a blowback from this conversation then she might as well get out all she wanted to say!

"You know what you did, Hayes? Nothing. Absolutely nothing, you sat there in my father's office and at his dining room table and heard what they were planning to do and you said nothing, did nothing! How can you be partners with a man like Michael Hansen? Especially now that you know he will stop at nothing to make a dollar or to get his way? I know you didn't make this deal, but to sit there and silently let it happen? It makes you just as guilty as they are in my eyes." Makia picked up her gloves and wraps and quickly left his office, once again wiping away angry tears.

## Chapter 3

Hayes silently put the supplies back inside his first aid kit, Makia's tear stained face and words rolling over and over again in his mind. What was it that Michael and her parents did to her that was so bad that now she thought he was part of it? He had no clue what she was talking about but he was going to find out, either Michael or Jason Sallow had some explaining to do.

"Hey man, what's going? You have a good workout?" Michael asked Hayes as he entered Michael's office without knocking, an hour and half later.

Hayes took quick notice of the fact that Michael quickly turned his back to him and appeared to be zipping up his pants while his personal assistant was sitting behind Michael's desk with a blush and a tousled blouse.

"Oh my bad, man. I should have knocked or something but when I didn't see Michelle at the desk, I thought you had stepped out and was about to leave you a note," Hayes quickly explained, moving back to the door to leave.

Michelle was barely out of high school! Michael knew for a fact she just turned twenty! Gayle, the front desk receptionist was her aunt and had asked him to keep an eye on her niece because she was only working for them through summer.

"No worries, bro, stay. I'm here so what's up?.," Michael said, smiling over at him. He took a seat in his office chair as Michelle hurried out of the office with her eyes cast down.

Hayes watched her leave and looked back at Michael with a puzzled look on his face. "You know you're married, right?" he asked with a sarcastic smile, his blood already beginning to boil as he remembered Makia's emotional breakdown earlier. Did she find out he was cheating on her or something and thought he knew?

"Psssh, like that means any goddamn thing, it's a piece of paper, dude. An expensive ass piece of paper. Besides, I promised to love the bitch, but I don't remember saying a thing about being faithful. Maybe I did, I was so faded I really don't fucking remember," Michael admitted shamelessly, getting up to pour himself a drink.

Hayes knew he needed to leave, even though he could tell Michael was a bit tipsy. Hearing him refer to Makia as a bitch was taking him to a very dark place with some real fucked up thoughts. Still, he needed to know what Makia was accusing him of so instead he walked over and poured himself a taste of whiskey since it seemed to be loosening Michael's tongue anyway.

"If that's how you feel about marriage, bruh, why get married in the first damn place? You pressed Makia for almost two years to set a wedding date, if I remember correctly." Hayes walked over and sat on the leather sofa near the door to keep his distance from Michael, just in case he said some more slick shit about Makia. He couldn't understand why he was upset, especially since he didn't know her well, but he felt protective over her, nonetheless.

When she came apart earlier, all he wanted to do was find any way in his power to make it better. From the first time he met her, she always seemed so strong and confident and seeing her break down like that was really messing with him.

He brought the glass to his lips and realized his hands smelled like her. He didn't know if it was her soap or her lotion but the soft floral scent was playing with his nose.

"Shit, have you seen my wife? She's fine as hell, talented, and sophisticated, I would have been a damn fool to turn that offer down. Plus, the price was right and so I jumped on the shit immediately," Michael bragged with a slur in his words before joining Hayes on the couch.

Hayes blinked and shook his head, trying to comprehend what Michael just said. "Fuck you mean the price was right? Right for what? I know you a bit buzzed man but I'm talking about your wife not some business deal," he said, frowning over at Michael.

Michael gulped down the rest of his drink in big swallows. "And I'm talking about both!"

Hayes looked at Michael and set his glass on the table before standing. "On that note, I'm going to head out, man. Be easy on that drink, you still do have an image to uphold, Mr. CEO," Hayes spat. He rushed across the hall to his receptionist.

"Hey Sanchez, I'm going to be out for the rest of the day. You know the routine, forward me the important calls and if it's quiet in an hour, you can leave." He was beyond pissed. The longer he worked with Michael, the grimier he found out the bastard was. What kind of mail order bride bullshit did this motherfucker get him into?

"Hayes, that girl you told me to be on the lookout for? She's here for the 4 o'clock boxing class," Reggie, co-owner of the gym peeked his head into his office and told him.

It had been three weeks since she was here. At first he was doubting she would even come back to his gym because of how she felt about him, but now considering all he knew about her, he thought there was a good chance she would. Hayes wasn't trying to be a creeper but he had his PI look into her. After what he found out he just needed to get her alone so he could clear his name, at least that's what he kept telling himself.

"Good looking out. Do me a favor, let me know when that class is over and do your best to keep an eye out for her, cool?" Hayes asked, standing up and moving from behind his desk.

"Cool. You good, Hayes? You look pissed, what this girl do to you, man? She owe you some money or something?" Reggie asked, moving out the doorway so Hayes could get by.

"Naw man, nothing like that. If anything, I owe her," Hayes answered and continued down to the men's locker room. He quickly changed into his gym shorts and beat up Cozumel t-shirt before pulling his gloves and wraps out of his locker. He frowned down at his knuckles, annoyed that they were still a little swollen after his visit with Jason Sallow. His weak ass had the nerve to tear up and then blame the entire thing on his wife as if he didn't skin and grin right along with Evelyn and Michael.

Now, Hayes had his attorneys and private investigator trying to find the contract between Michael and the Sallows and the presumed prenup Makia was forced to sign. They had instructions to go over everything with a fine-tooth comb to get Makia out of the marriage unscathed once they found them. All of this would be so much easier if he could somehow convince Makia to trust him and let him help her.

When Michael showed up in his office two days after he let his secret slip, he tried to tell Hayes it was just the alcohol talking and asked him to keep it between them. He even tried to suck up to him by saying Hayes was like a brother to him. Hayes had shaken his hand, even pulled him in for a bro hug to pretend they were still cool, knowing good and damn well he was making moves to sever all business ties with Michael Hansen for good.

It's funny that when you're young, no one wants to take you seriously until it's too late. In the eight years he had worked with Michael, he had worked his ass off and all of his investing and business ventures were starting to pay off. At 27 years old, his net worth was about to hit 1.9 billion so he had the means to help Makia win this fight against Michael.

He watched her from the doorway, just like the last time she was at the gym. Taking a big drink of water, she tapped her Air Pod to start her music and started fighting the same heavy bag she used before. He made sure the room was empty before making his way over to her. Her curly hair was pulled into a ponytail on the top of her head and, like last time, she was wearing leggings and a sports bra with a tank top over it, all in orchid purple.

The closer he got to her, the more he could smell the soft, floral scent he was beginning to think was just her own naturally. She rolled her eyes and her face was set in anger when she looked up and saw him coming her way. Her hits landed on the bag harder and louder the closer he got. When he was right up on her, he noticed the bluish-green bruise under her left eye.

"What the fuck?" he asked in alarm. When she stopped hitting the bag and faced him head on, he saw it was even worse as the blood vessels in her eye were busted too.

"Like you don't know," she quipped and got back in the stance to start to hit the bag again.

Hayes reached and stopped the bag from swinging with

one hand and used the other to softly move her face into the light.

"Michael did this?" Hayes asked angrily, he fought against the dark thoughts pressing hard against his common sense and voice of reason.

"Yep, fucking coward waited until I went to sleep and snuck in my room." Makia rolled her eyes against the tears that threatened to fall and pulled her head away from his touch.

"You got that shit right! Only a coward of a man would hit a woman but I gotta ask why you are shooting daggers at me like I did it?" He reached out and lightly touched her face again, all the while wanting to make Michael's eye look as blue and busted as hers.

Makia pushed the tear rolling down her cheek away impatiently, glaring up at him. "Because you went to see my father and my father told him what you said!" she yelled with a trembling lip.

Hayes frowned in confusion, picked up her water bottle, and took her by the hand leading her to his office. He could tell she was on the brink of breaking down again. Once he made sure she was okay, he moved to sit behind his desk so he wouldn't be inclined to touch her and cause anymore Michael-Hayes associations in her mind.

"What did your father say I said?" he asked her quietly, his voice low and tight.

She cleared her throat and pulled her gloves off to wipe her face. "Michael said you told my father I told you about their business arrangement and that you demanded to be compensated for being left out of it. This was his payback for me embarrassing him by telling his business," she answered sadly with her head down.

"You have got to be fucking kidding me! Makia, I know you have no reason in this world to trust me but I promise you I had no idea what was going down that night. Michael brought me along to look at the state of your father's company and to consider if the bailout was a profitable move for Hansen, period. I would have never been involved in something as heinous as the shit they did to you and tried to do to your sister.

"And while I will admit that I did go see your father, I went there on the intel I got straight from the horse's mouth. Michael was drinking in his office and let it slip a little bit ago. When I got there your father tried to deny everything and shifted all the blame to your mother. He said she was the one who made him marry you off to Michael and sell him your studio and grandmother's house.

"He told me everything, Makia. It was like he was Catholic and I was the priest. He even talked about how they have your trust tied to the stipulation that you must have a child in the next seven years or you don't get a dime. If you fail to deliver it reverses back to him and your mom. I could tell he was pretty proud of that part of the deal, he bragged about it for about ten minutes. It was right about then that I got tired of his whiny ass voice and tried to knock his whole face off," Hayes recounted his bad deed and held up his busted knuckles as proof.

Makia felt like she was about to faint, trying to process what he just said. Her trust was her safety net, her end game when they found a loophole to get her out of this nightmare. There was no way in hell she would have a baby with that ogre and have to deal with him for the rest of her life! Yeah, her parents and Michael mentioned seven years and a baby but she went over the contracts and prenup with a fine-tooth comb twice and a baby was never mentioned so she thought they gave up on it long ago.

"Look Makia, I know you hate me as much as you hate them and maybe you should, for me being so damn clueless about this, but you are going to have to find a way past that and let me help you, feel me? I know you don't have the means to fight this alone and it's killing me that this is happening to you, so you need to get used to the idea of me being in your corner," Hayes informed her watching her reaction closely.

"But why, Hayes? Why in God's name would you want to help me? You don't even know me," Makia asked, shrugging and grabbing her water bottle.

"You're right I don't, but I do know Michael, and due to that fact, I want to help you. I have always wondered how you two ended up married, especially when it was more than obvious you hated his ass from the minute you met him. This is some grimy shit he and your parents pulled. Like I said before I'm not asking for your trust, I'm telling you I'm helping you get out of this. Now it's up to you how difficult you are at accepting my assistance, it's happening regardless, baby girl. No one should have to endure what he is obviously putting you through, Makia," Hayes reasoned, looking over at her and trying to ignore how her black eye made him feel.

He could tell she was thinking about what he just said, really thinking about it. He sat quietly watching her as she undid her wraps and dropped them on top of her gloves before looking over at him again, taking a deep breath.

"Okay, Hayes, you want to help me? Cool, then help me, where do we begin?"

## Chapter 4

"**W**here the fuck you been, Makia? Why the hell are you getting in so damn late?" Michael raged as soon as she stepped into the house, a few days after her talk with Hayes.

Makia dropped her house keys in the lead crystal bowl she kept by the door and sighed impatiently. "Michael, is your phone broken?" she asked, her face already getting hot from anger as she glared at him.

He pulled his phone out of his pocket and held it up to her, gritting his teeth angrily. "No. What does that have to do with how late you are, Makia?"

"Hmm, interesting. So where the fuck were you when I had to be rushed to the hospital, Michael? The ER nurse and I both tried calling you several times," Makia stated, setting her purse and gym bag at her feet.

The shit she just had to endure was the last fucking straw as far as she was concerned. She had been in so much pain when she got to the hospital, she could barely stand and she honestly thought she was dying.

It wasn't until her test results came back positive for

chlamydia and gonorrhea that she went from scared to pissed. The doctor said it was so bad that the ultrasound showed possible permanent tubal scarring, she had to follow up with another ultrasound, this time with contrast to be sure.

"Emergency room? What the hell happened, Makia? Are you okay, baby?" He rushed over, taking her by the shoulders to see where she might be injured.

She pushed Michael's hands off of her and side stepped him, the maggoty feeling she always got when he touched her was even more pronounced than usual. "Do me a favor, okay, Michael? Stop acting like you give a fuck about anything or anybody but your damn self. I came into this knowing what it was so don't switch up now. We both know the only reason why you are even coming at me is because of your own guilt and where you've been tonight, you are just heated you beat me home for a change. No need to feel that way though because you are free to fuck, screw, lick, suck and bump uglies with whomever you choose, whenever you choose, I really don't give a fuck because honestly its one less time I have to deal with your failed attempts at sex and bottom line, *I don't care*! It's when you put my health and well-being at risk that I take issue with it, you drippy dick fucker."

One of his sweaty hands connected with her cheek, while the other one closed around her throat as he pushed her up against the door bringing her slightly off of her feet.

"Once again, you're mistaking my kindness for weakness with that slick ass mouth of yours! Who would have thought you would need two lessons in the same goddamn week? I told you the last time I had to jack your ass up to remember who the fuck you're talking to. I strongly suggest your little prissy ass apologizes, takes some of the sass out of your mouth, and tells me just what the fuck you're talking about before I snap your fucking neck!" he growled with his face inches from hers.

She was so numb to the mental and physical pain of being

married to Michael that she didn't even cry anymore. Now, him putting his hands on her again had been the cue she'd been waiting for. Usually she avoided the confrontation whenever possible but the minute she got those results she was ready to beat the shit out of Michael.

"You want to know what the fuck I'm talking about, Michael? Huh, Michael? You gave me not one, but two sexually transmitted diseases! You put my health in danger playing Russian Roulette with your life, *you dirty dick motherfucker*!" She reached beside her and grabbed the lead crystal bowl that held her keys and smashed it on the side of his head. He quickly let her go and dropped to the ground, grabbing his head that was now pouring blood.

She picked up her purse and gym bag and kicked him in the ribs as she passed him and saw him trying to get up. "From this day forward, you will not lay a fucking finger on me or every time you do I will march into your fucking office with all the bruises on my face, the fingerprints on my neck, and the cuts on my hands on display so they can all see what a sick fucking pig you are! How many times do you think people will tolerate it until the police are called so they can drag your stupid ass to jail? Yeah, yeah, I know you'd be out in an hour. I still can't leave because you will take everything away from me, Sage and Grandma Lo, blah, blah, blah, but by then your business partners and associates will know what a bullying asshole you really are!

"And if not them, let's not forget all the wives! You know, the ones who positively adore me and all the work Sage and I did for the Women's Center and Domestic Abuse Prevention Foundation fundraising gala last spring? Wasn't that the one that landed you the two-page write-up in Forbes magazine, Michael? You know, maybe it is time for me to take them up on their lunch invite and catch up, I do have most of tomorrow free. How long do you think it will take before your little fan club is as tired of your ass as I am?" she spat, snatching the heavy wooden front door open to leave the house.

Michael stumbled to his feet and tried to close the door, but she was able to fight him for control of it and step out on their front porch.

"Just where the hell do you think you're going, Makia?" he demanded, trying to keep his balance as he held onto the door.

"To stay the night at the studio because if I stay here with you, I will spend the rest of the night trying my damndest to beat the fuck outta you. Don't even think of trying anything stupid, I meant what I said and I will expose all your shit!" Makia stormed down the stairs to her car and peeled out of the driveway before he managed to cross the threshold of the front door.

---

"Hello! Anybody home?" Makia called out as she walked into her grandmother's house a few days later.

"Hey Sissy! We're out back on the patio, we're grilling your favorite tonight!"

No matter how busy Sage and she were, they always got together for dinner on Sunday evenings with their grandmother Lola. Makia stepped out on the covered patio in her sunglasses, heavy makeup, and a scarf tied around her bruised neck, hoping she could hide the injuries from her family. The tiny cut on her lip his slap had caused was just about healed and hidden under tinted lip gloss.

She held up the Sage-requested German chocolate cake for dessert and the smell of grilled chicken and vegetables reminded her she hadn't eaten all day. Kebabs were one of her absolute favorites, the other was chicken wraps. She knew from experience if they were grilling, that meant her grandmother's smoked bacon and cheddar deviled eggs and cucumber salad were both chilling in the fridge, too. Her stomach was suddenly screaming to get a taste.

"My two favorite ladies! How are you Grandma Lo?" She rushed over and hugged her grandmother from behind her wheelchair, kissing her on the cheek.

Makia's smile dropped when her grandmother pulled her glasses from her face slowly and led Makia in front of her so they were facing each other. For someone 78 years old who had recently suffered a mild stroke, she was still very astute.

"He hit you again," her grandmother stated quietly, moving Makia's head from side to side looking at her bruised face before pulling the scarf away from her neck.

"Sage, baby, go in the bathroom and grab me that salve on the bottom shelf in the medicine cabinet. Makia and I will keep an eye on the food," her grandmother instructed, her big brown eyes filling with tears. She had Makia sit down next to her so she could see her face closer. Sage took the cake from Makia's hands and walked to the kitchen.

"Makia, you have to leave him. We will figure something else out, I can't see you like this anymore!" Lola said as tears rolled down her face.

"Grandma, we talked about this and you know that is not an option right now. He has the money to come after us no matter where we go, and even if one of us won the lottery tomorrow, it's not enough for the three of us to get away from here," Makia reasoned, reaching out and wiping the tears from her grandmother's face.

Sage came back with the salve, two warm towels, and old makeup remover and set it all on Lola's lap before sitting down on the other side of Makia. Tears sprang to Sage's eyes, too when Lola pulled Makia's blouse to the side and exposed her bruised neck and began to wipe the makeup off her face so they could use the salve.

"Sissy, he tried to strangle you! I can see his fingerprints!

Makia, you can't go back to that house!" Sage sobbed and grabbed the other towel to help their grandmother clean Makia up.

"Who would have thought trusting my only child would land me here, and that same child would subject his daughter to this kind of abuse and all for money?" Her grandmother mused with a sigh as she tended to Makia.

"None of us could have seen something like this coming but here we are and I will be okay. You both know if I look like this, he looks five times worse, so trust me okay? This will all be over and sooner than you think. Now can we get me all patched up so we can eat? I'm starving!" Makia told them, grabbing both into a hug.

---

Makia marched into the house carrying a storage container with her leftovers from dinner. In spite of how it began, she had the best time with her family and her sides hurt from laughing so hard.

She could hear voices coming from Michael's office as she made her way to the kitchen. Her goal was to put her food in the fridge and get up to her room before he even realized she was home. She was in no mood to see him and his brand of BS, especially after her having such a good time with Sage and her grandmother. Happy moments were pretty rare for her these days and she wanted to bask in it a little longer.

To add to her good mood, she had outsmarted him yet again. The day after their fight, he was drunk and kicked her door in when she came home and locked him out of her room. Luckily, no blows were thrown that night, just him whining and wanting her to see that it took twenty-two stitches to close the wound on the side of his head. Michael was an enigma that way, he was only violent towards her when he was sober.

The next day he woke her up early and ordered her to arrange to have the broken door replaced before anyone saw it. She found a company that made custom doors and once she told the company 'money is no object' they came and installed her custom-made door which was a replica of the previous door, but with metal inside, all within 24 hours.

"Ah, you're here, I thought I heard you walk in. You bring me a plate this time or something?" Michael asked, coming into the kitchen behind her and eyeballing her container of leftovers.

She rolled her eyes heavenward and sighed before glaring over her shoulder in his direction and putting her leftovers in the fridge.

"Like that would ever happen," she mumbled under her breath, praying he wasn't about to start with her again. "Yep I'm here, what's up?" She asked as politely as she could force herself to, turning around to face him with her arms folded. She watched his plastic smile fade as he took in all the bruises on her face and neck. Without all of her makeup on, she knew how bad they looked.

"Hayes is here, I wanted him here for something I need to discuss with you, why don't you run upstairs and put some makeup on and meet me in my office in ten minutes?" Michael suggested, obviously uncomfortable seeing the full result of his handiwork.

Makia's stomach dropped in alarm, why was he here? Her voice of reason was screaming in her head 'See? You were right he is just as grimy as Michael!' Even with a million questions rolling around in her head and a small feeling of defeat, she still moved around the island and started to walk proudly with her head held high to Michael's office.

He caught up with her and stopped her just as she reached the closed door. "Didn't I just tell you to go upstairs and put some makeup on and meet us down here in ten minutes?" he gritted out, squeezing her upper arm.

Makia looked from his hand to his face and back again like he was crazy. "And didn't I tell you that you are never to lay another unwelcome finger on me again? Now, your business partner is on the other side of this door, I can either give him a show complete with crocodile tears and let him draw the right conclusion of why my face looks like this or I can spin a little tale to save your image and your ass once again. Now you've got about five seconds," she whispered fiercely before smiling up at him with her most hateful smile.

Michael quickly let her arm go and opened the door to escort her into his office. Hayes was sitting in front of Michael's desk and was slightly turned as he was talking to another handsome man she had never seen before with bulging muscles, dressed in an all-black suit who was standing near the window. Their conversation trailed off and ceased all together when she walked in and they saw her face and neck. Makia's hostile gaze locked with Hayes' curious one, while she settled in the chair next to him just as her phone chimed to let her know she had a message.

"Sweetheart, would you like anything to drink?" Michael asked her, walking over to the wet bar to pour himself a drink.

"No thanks, you know I don't drink and I hate to appear rude but can you please tell me what this is all about so I can go to my room? I have a lot to prepare for tomorrow, I have a speaking engagement at George Mason," Makia answered, folding her hands in her lap, still smiling.

Michael shot her a warning look over his shoulder before going back to pouring his drink. She could feel Hayes' eyes moving across her face and neck taking in her injuries.

"I wasn't aware of that but I know you need your rest, so let's get right into it. As you know, Hayes is my senior business partner and right-hand man so needless to say, when he saw my injuries and now sees yours, he was concerned with our safety after that failed home invasion attempt and suggested a security detail," Michael informed her with a villainous grin.

Makia sat straight up in her chair and glared at both Michael and Hayes, opening her mouth in protest when Michael raised his hand to silence her.

"Before you say no it's already done, Makia. Hayes has already arranged it for us. Allow me to introduce you to Reggie, your new bodyguard. He will drive you around and be with you wherever you go, including the studio."

Makia was so pissed, her ears were ringing! This was helping her? This motherfucker convinced Michael's controlling ass to get her another fucking bodyguard? He just made things ten times worse! There was no way in hell she was going to tolerate this shit again!

"As we previously discussed, Michael, I don't want or need a bodyguard," Makia ground out, feeling like she was about to explode.

"I know but that was then, things have changed now. My biggest concern is keeping you safe. Just look at what some monster did to you, I'm afraid this is not up for negotiation," Michael simpered, his eyes threatening and low.

"I see. Well, Hayes I can't thank you enough for all of your *help*. I don't know where I would be without it, " she snapped, rising to her feet and glaring daggers at Hayes.

He looked up at her but remained seated. "Anytime Makia, you'll have to trust me when I say Reggie is the best man for the job," Hayes said and finished the last bit of his drink.

"Good to know I will be protected from *the monsters*. Let's hope in our case we are the exception not the rule." She continued to treat Michael and Hayes to her glare.

"What do you mean 'exception not the rule', Makia?" Michael asked her, swirling his drink in his glass.

"Oh you know how it goes, Michael. In almost every scary

movie you find out the monsters you don't know aren't nearly as scary as the monsters you do know. Reggie, I look forward to working with you. Good night, gentlemen." She nodded to all three of them before turning to leave.

"Makia?" Michael called her name softly, smiling triumphantly that he finally got what he wanted.

"Yes?" she answered with her back to them, tears of frustration starting to sting her eyes.

"Please don't be angry with Hayes, he only wanted to help and it's all for your safety. Please make sure to send Reggie your complete schedule for the week and sleep well, beautiful."

Makia nodded and left his office, looking down at her phone as she rushed back through the house towards her room. She paused as she stepped inside her room.

She had two new text messages. The most recent one was from Sage telling her she loved her and to be careful. The second was a text message from a new number over an hour ago that read, "Relax, this is all part of the plan."

---

He could taste blood in his mouth and knew it was because of how hard he was biting the inside of his cheek. Every time he looked at Michael, all he could see was Makia's bruised and battered face and he got heated all over again. The man was pure garbage for doing that shit to her.

"Hayes did you hear what I said, man?" Michael asked, leaning forward on his desk and still grinning.

Hayes lifted his eyes to Michael's. "Nah sorry, didn't catch it." He shrugged indifferently, Hayes being the center of attention in any room they were both in, bothered Michael more than anything.

"I said good looking out! Now I can keep even closer tabs on her sneaky ass!" Michael boasted, throwing his drink back.

Hayes leaned to the side in his chair, stroking his chin thoughtfully. "Tabs?" he mused quietly, nodding at Michael.

"Hell yeah tabs! Fuck you thought? I told you I don't trust her ass or that dyke sister of hers, they are up to something," Michael said, stepping over to make another drink.

"Interesting, and here I thought it was about protecting your wife, especially after seeing her face. Silly me," Hayes smirked, standing to take his glass back to the wet bar.

Michael was watching him silently, his jaw bunching in anger. Hayes cast a lazy smile Michael's way when he stepped up next to him, he wished this weak ass punk would try to step to him.

"What are you trying to say, Hayes? That you care more about my wife's safety than I do or something?" Michael snapped, puffing up angrily.

"Nah, bruh, I ain't said shit. You did." Hayes set his empty glass on the bar and signaled for Reggie to follow him out.

"Hey hold up, Hayes. My bad, man, all this home invasion shit got me tripping. I know all you're trying to do is look out for me like you always do, we good?" Michael asked, walking up to Hayes, offering him his fist to bump.

"We good. Looks like Makia already sent Reggie her itinerary; he will be here to pick her up at 7:30 in morning so she can make it to her speaking engagement." Hayes fist bumped Michael and left with Reggie.

"Ay man, what the fuck was that about? She ain't sent me shit!" Reggie whispered as he climbed into the passenger side of Hayes' Escalade.

"You saw that girl's face, maybe knowing you're going to be around from now on and will be here first thing in the morning will encourage Michael to keep his damn hands to himself while I work on getting her away from that piece of shit," Hayes answered, chucking his chin in Michael's direction. He was standing in the doorway sipping his drink watching them leave.

"Bruh, it took all the strength in my body not to fuck his shit all the way up! I have zero respect or patience for any man who would put his hands on a woman, especially like that. Peep game though, me being there during the day doesn't stop him from fucking with her at night and this may all be for nothing if you can't get her on board with it. I mean, bro she looked at you like she hates your ass more than him!" Reggie reasoned, chuckling a little.

"Yeah, I know but let me worry about that. I'll convince her to play nice somehow, let's get the detail started for now. I'm moving things around in my mind on how to convince Michael you need to be a live in, would you be cool with that if I can make it happen?" Hayes asked Reggie, pulling onto the highway towards downtown.

"Yeah man, whatever it takes, I told you I'm in. Remember, I got you, Bro!"

Hayes held out his fist for Reggie to pound, with a smile. The only person he knew he could trust 100% was his brother Reggie. They had different fathers but none of that mattered to them.

Because Hayes was such a private person, no one knew much about his family other than what he wanted them to know. If you Googled him, all that came up was his accolades in business and the fact he was his father's only child.

Hayes had inherited his savvy business sense from his biological father who killed himself when Hayes was five years old. His mother wouldn't talk about it at all, other than to assure him it had nothing to do with him.

His calculated execution and focus on all tasks was taught to him and Reggie by his stepfather Rydwan Purcell, attorney at law. Hayes had mad respect for Ryd from day one, he made sure Hayes understood he knew he wasn't his father biologically but he would always be his son. When Reggie was born, Ryd drove that point home and even took the time to do special things with Hayes to make sure he knew nothing had changed.

Reggie studied Hayes' profile with a knowing smile. He knew his brother better than anybody and he wasn't buying that 'I just want to help her, that's it' line he kept trying to feed him.

"So, tell me again why you're doing all of this?" he asked Hayes, trying to act nonchalant and fighting the smile tugging at his face.

Hayes looked over at Reggie before focusing his attention back to the road. "Man, Reggie, I already told your ass I just want to help her, that's it! Why do you keep bringing it up? Damn!"

Reggie nodded, bringing his fist to his mouth and faking a cough to cover up his chuckles. "My bad, Hay, I musta forgot."

Hayes pulled off the highway and drove to the gym, squeezing the wheel tight until he pulled up next to Reggie's pickup truck.

"Man, fuck you, Reggie! She's married and drive Regina's sexy ass tomorrow, you need to look legit," Hayes instructed, referring to Reggie's new gunmetal gray Bentley Flying Spur he named Regina.

"Aww shit! I was going to drive pops' Benzo but you right, my pretty girl is even better!" Reggie called over his shoulder, walking over to his truck.

"Ay man, thanks again for helping with this. I know it's a lot to ask, I owe you one," Hayes said, putting his car in park.

"No worries, I got you, big bro! I'll keep your lady safe, man," Reggie teased, starting up his truck and quickly pulling out of the gym parking lot.

"Fuck you, Reggie!" Hayes screamed out his car window. Reggie's truck horn sounded in response making him laugh.

He ran his hand down his face and tried to get Makia's bruised face out of his head as he dialed her number from the TracFone he was using to communicate with her. He needed to explain about Reggie before he got there in the morning.

"Hello?" Makia's soft voice answered curiously, echoing in his car like she was there with him. She sounded so calm and sweet, nothing like the jab throwing, glaring woman he knew.

"Hey, it's Hayes, are you near him right now?" he asked her, again hating the fact that he hadn't moved fast enough to prevent Michael from hitting her again.

"No Sage, like I told you I won't be at the studio until tomorrow afternoon so you don't have to pick me up anything for breakfast."

Hayes frowned for a minute in confusion when he got a text from Makia saying, *"Can't talk talk, he has cameras everywhere, including my bathroom. Now he gets to watch me when I'm gone too thanks to your ass!"*

He sighed, shaking his head, "It's not like that Makia, I convinced him to hire Reggie so we can keep an eye on Michael not you, so he can keep you safe. And if he's watching you, won't he get suspicious that you're texting?"

"Nothing really, Sissy, just adding the talking points for tomorrow to my notes app. What are you doing?" Makia said as she texted, *"I have lived in this prison for a year and half now, I have my ways around his controlling ass."*

"So check it, I'm going to send you a fake itinerary. I need you to email Reggie, just cut and paste it so it's coming from your email and he's going to forward it to Michael. I'm thinking him believing he has you securely under his thumb will make him back off a little bit. Reggie is going to drive you to meet with me after your lecture tomorrow; I want to go over a few things I found out with you. I know you still don't trust me and that's cool, actions speak louder than words and one day you will," Hayes promised, checking his regular phone. He had a text from Michael, his bitch ass thanking him again for getting the bodyguard.

"That sounds like fun Sissy, I hate that I'm going to miss them, you know that's my favorite group of all time. See if you can't get an autograph for me, okay? I'm going to turn in though, I set my alarm for six and you and I both know morning comes too soon on Mondays," she said, sighing and faking a yawn for emphasis.

*"Michael goes down for breakfast at 6 and leaves for work by 7. What time is Reggie coming?"* Her text read.

"He'll be there at 7:30 sharp, he wants to make sure to get you to George Mason on time. Do you think you'll be okay until then or should I send him earlier?" Hayes closed his eyes and saw her face behind his eyelids, even bruised she was one of the most beautiful women he had ever met. He hated the way his body responded every time she spoke.

"Oh okay, that's fine. I promised Grandma I would pick her up from the salon anyway, so by the time I drive her home and head back downtown your session should be over, sound good?" Makia answered with a real yawn this time.

*"7:30 is fine, are you 100% sure you can trust him? Michael can be very persuasive with the amount of money he is willing to pay to get what he wants. Also I'm good (for a few days anyway), I'm pretty sure he doesn't have it in him to have another lead crystal bowl smashed upside his head. One thing to always remember about me, Hayes, if I look bad I make sure his bullying ass looks bad too, worse if I can."*

"Damn! I see you Makia, that's what's up! I was wondering what you hit his ass with! And I trust Reggie with my life, Michael could offer him all the money he has in the bank and Reggie wouldn't budge, I promise you. So I will plan on seeing you after your lecture tomorrow then, cool?" he asked, grinning proudly.

"I love you too, Sissy, and I'll text you when I'm on my way, just in case you need me to pick you up something to eat. We haven't had wraps in a while, so think about it and let me know okay?"

*"Okay thanks, anything else?"*

"Nothing that can't wait until tomorrow, just be sure to always delete our messages. Sleep well, Makia," he said softly, putting his car back in drive. He actually felt a little sad when her number disappeared from his dashboard display, indicating she hung up. His phone pinged one last time.

*"You too. Thank you, Hayes."*

## Chapter 5

"Look at my wifey this morning!" Michael commented loudly as Makia stepped into the kitchen the following morning. "Looking all smart and sassy and shit, can't hardly tell you even have a mark on you," he sneered, glaring at her as he finished his coffee.

She had dragged her feet for as long as she could before coming down to breakfast, so why the fuck was he still here? She asked God forgiveness everyday but she truly hated this man.

"Michael, you know good and damn well I don't wear makeup unless I'm going out with you to one of those stuffy ass dinners or I'm covering up your handiwork, which we both know is the only reason I am wearing it today. Now before you go trying to invent a reason to start with me this morning, why don't you ponder that for a moment or maybe even think about keeping your hands to yourself like most big boys do," Makia suggested, giving him the evil eye before smiling thankfully at their chef for her acai bowl.

She had no idea what the woman's name was because she was one of many. Once Michael showed his true colors or had his way with them, they always quit, so sadly, she stopped trying to get to know them at all.

"You embarrassed the shit out of me last night, Makia. All you had to do is go upstairs and do exactly what you did this morning! You made me look bad and I didn't appreciate it, so don't let it happen again," Michael threatened, rising from his seat at the table.

"You embarrassed yourself, Michael! It was late, putting on makeup is a process and I wasn't about to put it on just to take it off twenty minutes later and may I remind you I didn't give myself these marks!" Makia snapped defiantly, glaring up at him as he moved closer and stood over her.

He leaned in closely and lightly touched her face. "Hmm, true. I'll make sure to only punish you with body shots from now on," he threatened and tried to kiss her softly on the cheek.

She quickly moved her head and he grabbed her chin aggressively. "You just love pissing me off, don't you, Makia?" he growled just as the doorbell rang.

She heard one of the servants' hurried steps to the door and a deep baritone voice echoing in the foyer before moving towards the dining room.

"Saved by the bell," he muttered and let her face go just as Reggie walked into the room in all black again, a small smile on his face.

"Good morning, Mr. Hansen. Makia. Sorry to interrupt but Hayes informed me first thing this morning of the change in your schedule. There is also a detour on the way to Mason, so with the new route we're taking, we need to leave sooner rather than later," Reggie said referring to them the way Michael had insisted. Somehow he felt calling Makia by her first name and him by his last name emphasized who was truly in charge which was some of the dumbest shit Reggie ever heard, to be honest.

He could feel the tension as he stepped deeper into the room to shake hands with Michael. He wanted to break that shit seeing how upset Makia already looked when it was only seven in the morning.

Makia quickly pushed her chair back and rushed up to her room to grab her purse, portfolio, and her phone so they could leave. She wondered how the hell Reggie knew to come early before she noticed a new text from Hayes' burner phone.

*"My assistant is covering Michael's desk until he hires a new one and he mentioned Michael called to say he was running late today. Reggie is on his way."*

Makia deleted the message with a small smile on her face as she made her way back to the dining room where Michael and Reggie were talking in hushed tones.

"You ready, love? You know you never told me what subject you are lecturing in today," Michael stated, looking in her eyes and moving in closer to her. She could tell he was going to try to kiss her to basically mark his territory with Reggie. His eyes were almost daring her to stop him when Reggie stepped around Michael and grabbed her portfolio from her hands.

"Ready, Makia? Just got another alert and the detour is backed up now, too. We need to leave now to get you there on time. Mr. Hansen, it was a pleasure to see you again and don't worry, she's in good hands. No one, and I do mean no one, will be able to get close to your wife without her permission." Reggie's friendly smile and jovial mannerisms had been quickly replaced with an all business, take no shit demeanor.

"To answer your question I am speaking on the villains throughout art history. Seems appropriate, don't you think? And for the record, this whole bodyguard thing is both stupid and unnecessary and you know it!" Makia snapped looking pissed off and annoyed at both Reggie and Michael as she snatched her water bottle from the table and turned to leave.

Reggie moved to the side to let Makia storm out of the

dining room and fell in step behind her for a few steps before pausing and turning back to Michael. "One more thing, Mr. Hansen, you might want to wash the makeup up off your hand before you ruin that Armani suit. It's fire, by the way," Reggie added before jogging to catch up with Makia to open the door for her and escort to his car.

Reggie dropped into the driver's seat of his car and pulled out of the driveway as Makia stared out the window in annoyance at Michael who was smiling his predatory smile from the porch.

"Thank you for that, and for coming early," Makia said with a small smile once they were past her house.

"Anytime. Trust me, he won't be able to even blink too close to you if you don't want him to while I'm around and no problem with the change of plans, it gave me the opportunity to see what Regina can really do," he said, looking at her in the rearview mirror.

"Regina?" Makia asked while pulling her compact from her purse to check her makeup and make sure all the bruises were still covered up.

"Yeah, Regina. Oh my bad, I didn't introduce y'all yet. Makia, this is my one and only love, Regina. Regina, this is Makia, she's gonna be hanging out with us for a while," Reggie answered and made the introductions.

Makia chuckled and dropped her compact back in her purse. "So let me get this straight. You, Reggie, named your car Regina?" Makia asked, pointing to him and around the interior of the car.

"Yep, Regina is a fly ass name because it's the female version of my name and in time you will know how fly I am, I promise you! For now you might want to buckle up and hold on because me and my girl about to get real close, hell yeah!" he said, grinning from ear to ear as he pulled onto the highway and pressed his foot harder on the gas pedal. Regina's engine roared happily in response.

———

"Now where are we, exactly?" Makia asked, walking up the steps to a beautiful house surrounded on all sides by trees and hedges a few hours after her speaking engagement. She noticed everything was so lush, pretty, and alive with color.

Reggie opened the door for her and escorted her inside. After talking to her for the last few hours and sitting in on her talk, Reggie was really impressed with Makia. You would never suspect she was going through all she was behind the scenes, although, since he did know what was going on, some of her tongue-in-cheek comedy was not missed.

"Paradise," Reggie answered, walking her through the house and out to the backyard of the house he shared with Hayes.

They originally bought the house because it was out of the way and for its fully loaded amenities like the game room, movie theater, jacuzzi tubs in the master suites, and basketball court, but they kept the house for the privacy it provided and the dream backyard they designed and had built.

The patio was circular and housed a full kitchen, grilling station, bar, and a wood grill oven. Several sitting areas were scattered in groups and the entire area looked more like a family room than a backyard, though there were tall trees and bright flowers everywhere. They had an inground pool and lagoon with a retractable cover that was a stone walkway when the pool was covered. Hayes even had a second office built out there so he could enjoy the view while he worked.

"Damn, you ain't never lied! This place is beautiful, all that's missing is flower leis and Mai Tai's!" Makia stepped out to take it all in when movement at the pool had her tripping over her own feet and Reggie rushing forward to keep her upright.

Hayes was stepping out of the pool. Water rained down his muscular frame as he ascended the stone steps that led back to the patio. His swim trunks rode low on his waist because of the weight of the water in them and she could see the dark, coarse hairs that led to his groin peeking out.

His dreads he normally wore pulled back in a neat French braid down the back of his head were loose and hanging down his back. As he got closer, she could see the sprinkling of hair on his chest and an old scar on his side on his sun-kissed skin.

He lifted his head and came up short to see her standing there, her eyes dark and low as she watched him. "Oh, hi Makia," he said with an embarrassed smile. He quickly pulled his trunks up higher on his waist, snapping her out of her trance.

"What the hell are y'all trying to pull? What, did you think with Michael out of the way you could throw your hat in the ring? I seriously don't have time for this shit!" Makia snapped and stormed back inside the house, trying to get her hormones back in check. She had only had sex with one other man before Michael and not even that man had ever made her feel the way she was feeling right now.

"Makia! Makia, hold up! It's not like that, I forgot to let him know we were on our way out here after I ran you by the studio to change. This is all my fault, please don't take it out on Hayes, I bet he decided to get a swim in before we got here since he hadn't heard from me yet," Reggie quickly explained, looking embarrassed.

Makia looked at Reggie, trying to get the image of a wet and shirtless Hayes out of her head. Her first instinct was to tell Hayes the deal was off and have Reggie take her home but she had to admit she was in no position to do so. After she looked at her personal accounts last night, with how much she was paying her attorney, her half of the studio expenses, and helping her grandmother, she was putting more out than she was able to bring in and without her trust, they would not be able to survive when she finally got away from Michael. The truth was she needed Hayes' help now more than ever. Whether she trusted him or not, she had to take the chance.

"I get it and I'm sorry I snapped like that. I really owe Hayes an apology too, it was a knee jerk reaction. It's not his fault I'm in this mess but honestly, being on the defensive and not trusting anyone but my sister and grandmother is the only way I have survived this far," Makia explained, blushing in embarrassment at the most recent ugly accusation she had hurled at Hayes.

"Yeah that better be the last time you do, I don't like that shit. However, I would be surprised if you didn't question everything at this point and like I said before, you don't have to trust me to let me help you. Us help you." Hayes stepped into the room wearing a button down and shorts, his hair still down framing his handsome face, his feet bare as he gestured to indicate they were going back out on the patio.

"You guys eat?" Hayes asked Reggie, walking towards the fridge in the kitchen area.

"Have a seat, Makia. Get comfortable, you with the good guys now. And nah, bruh we headed straight out here after we left downtown to give y'all more time to discuss things," Reggie took the sparkling water Hayes sat on the counter and walked it and Makia's portfolio case over to her.

"Cool, in that case we can talk business over lunch, sound good?" Hayes asked Makia, watching her take a seat in the circle of high backed, black wicker chairs.

Makia thanked Reggie for the water quickly opening it and taking a long, refreshing drink. "Whatever works for you, I know you're taking time away from work to do this so I appreciate your time however I can get it," Makia said, refusing to look over at Hayes until her wayward thoughts calmed down a little more.

She pulled the copies of the marriage contracts, the prenup, and the paperwork regarding the sale of the studio and her grandmother's house she managed to make copies of when Michael accidently left his office open one night and set them on the table in front of her.

"Let me finish throwing this together and we can get down to business." Hayes pulled out all the ingredients he needed to make lunch and started to put it together.

"Cool, Imma get on this game for a second then. Call me when it's time to eat." Reggie stepped off the patio and walked past the pool to the dark glass doors on the other side of it.

Soon the serene quiet was disturbed with loud sounds of bass pumping music and gunfire from Grand Theft Auto.

Makia stared after him, finishing her drink. "I like him, he's cool people. If I have to have a bodyguard, I'm glad it's him, he's like a big brother or something," she said smiling, finally mustering the self-control needed to look at Hayes again.

Hayes looked up from the bowl he was mixing ingredients in and almost spilled it. Makia was smiling, not forced or fake like she normally did, but a genuine smile. She looked relaxed and truly happy for the first time since he met her and he thanked God he was able to witness the rare moment.

"What? Why are you looking at me like you have never seen me before in your life?" she asked him looking down at her sundress to make sure she hadn't spilled water down her front or something.

"Uh nothing, just thinking about the game plan that's all. So, lunch will be ready in about fifteen minutes, do you want another sparkling water to go with it?" Hayes asked, admonishing himself again for his strong attraction to Makia.

"Yeah that would be great and where can I wash my hands?" Makia asked, holding her hands up, smiling again.

The lower part of Hayes' body jerked in reaction, starting to grow hard as she walked over to the kitchen area. "Here, let me show you where the bathroom is, this sink has been tripping lately and I would hate for you to get all wet."

They both instantly stopped moving and looked at each other, their eyes wide in shock for a split second before they both started laughing. "That's what she said!" They both said in unison, laughing again.

"Nah man, don't tell me you watch "*The Office*"?" Hayes asked as he led her back inside the house and to one of the guest bathrooms.

Makia shrugged and walked past him to the bathroom door. "Fine. I won't tell you." She smirked and closed the door in his face.

Hayes turned around, shaking his head and readjusting his semihard erection. "I would hate for you to get all wet, who the fuck says stuff like that to a married woman? Especially one married to his fucking asshole business partner!" he mumbled, walking back onto the patio to put their food on the table.

"He would hate for me to get all wet? Shit, too late. I've been wet since his ass stepped out of that damn pool looking like Aqua man or some shit!" Makia said under her breath, washing her hands. She'd hand pumped so much hand soap into her hands that the entire sink was now full of soapy lather. She had officially lost her ever loving mind, she was literally attracted to Hayes Purcell! This was not good!

"Look, heffa get your head in the fucking game! This man is fine as hell, especially walking around barefoot with those sexy ass dreads of his... okay stop! Choose another thought, Makia! But goddamn he is fine though! Focus Makia, focus! This man is your ticket to freedom and the way to secure your family's future so get your damn hormones under control and let's handle business!" Makia whispered, arguing with herself in the bathroom mirror.

She took a few minutes to regain her composure, splashed cold water on her face, and opened the bathroom door with a sigh before walking back down the hall to meet with Hayes and Reggie on the patio again. They both stood up from the umbrella shaded patio table when they saw her come out. Hayes looked annoyed while Reggie sported an evil grin.

"You guys good?" she asked, walking over to grab her phone to check it and mute it before walking over to join them at the table.

"Yeah, we're good, Hayes just in his feelings," Reggie teased, sitting back down after Makia did. Hayes flopped back down in his chair glaring at Reggie before smiling at her.

"Yeah, sometimes Reggie likes to really try his luck, times like now. Anyway, I hope wraps are cool for lunch? While you were washing your hands, I realized it was kind of rude of me to assume you would like what I wanted for lunch but I remembered you mentioned it last night on the phone," Hayes inquired, pouring lemon water in the glass in front of him.

Makia eyeballed them curiously for a few more seconds before opening and pouring the bottle of sparkling water into her own glass. "How long have you two known each other? Overhearing you two on the phone earlier and how you've been acting since we got here I would swear you guys act like–"

"Brothers? Yeah we get that, a lot," Reggie said, smirking over at Hayes while taking a bite of his wrap.

Hayes put his own wrap down on his plate and glared at Reggie while he chewed his bite. "Keep it up," he warned looking annoyed and hostile.

"Okay then, Hayes should we talk about this plan of yours?" Makia asked, taking a bite of her own food. It was delicious! Everything melded together perfectly in that one bite! The cold chicken was grilled perfectly, the vegetables were fresh, and the sauce he made? She wanted to find the rest of it and eat it by itself with a spoon! She closed her eyes, took another bite, and actually moaned. Damn it all to hell the man could cook too! She was beginning to wonder if God hated her.

Hayes' hand stopped midway to his mouth, as he watched her in the throes of gastronomic ecstasy. Her tongue darted out and licked sauce from the corner of her mouth as she chewed, the action was hotwired to Hayes' groin and caused him to grow hard immediately. He dropped his napkin in his lap and cleared his throat.

"You good, Makia?" he choked out, while every muscle in his body screamed for him to snatch her out of that chair and really make her moan.

Makia opened her eyes slowly blushing with embarrassment as she focused on Hayes and Reggie. Hayes looked like he was in actual physical pain and Reggie had the same evil grin plastered on his face as he did when she came out of the bathroom.

"Nah, the question is are you alright Bro Bro?" Reggie laughed into his plate and Hayes looked like he was going to strangle him.

Makia took that tense moment to leave the table and go grab the folder she brought and hand it to Hayes, sitting back down in front of her plate, still blushing. "Look… um, sorry about that, it's just that chicken wraps are one of my favorite foods and I haven't had one in ages now that my sister Sage's fiancée Joslyn, just went vegan and the only day she eats meat and the foods her girlfriend says are bad for you is Sunday at my Grandma Lola's. If your grandmothers are anything like mine, you already know she ain't cooking wraps for Sunday dinner. And yours is good, like really good, and made me remember how much I missed having them. So yeah, that's why I just embarrassed myself moaning like an idiot over a chicken wrap," Makia explained before drinking all of her sparkling water and refusing to look at either one of them.

"We get it. Makia, you have to find joy wherever and whenever you can in life. That's what I'm always telling my– I mean telling Hayes here." Reggie quickly went back to eating when Hayes gave him another glare over the open folder.

Makia's eyes bounced back and forth between them curiously, checking off similarities between them in her mind. Even though Hayes was about three shades lighter and Reggie's fade looked way different than Hayes' dreads, they looked a lot alike.

"Hold up! Are you guys brothers?" Makia asked loudly, her eyes narrowing as she glared at them both. Hayes and Reggie exchanged alarmed looks before looking over at Makia.

"I told you to just tell her from the jump, Hayes. Now look at you over there looking guilty as hell," Reggie said, shaking his head knowingly and shoving the last bite of his wrap in his mouth.

"And I told you to let me handle it! Damn, Reg! If your goofy ass wasn't always teasing about me being attracted to her and shit she would have never picked up on it!" Hayes snapped, slamming her folder on the table so hard the dishes rattled.

Makia jumped, pushing away from the table and was in a fighting stance before she had time to even think about where she was. When she realized what she just did, she covered her face in embarrassment and rushed back to the guest bathroom.

Reggie looked from her retreating back to Hayes. "Damn, I'm sorry, bro, I was just fucking with you because I know you're catching feelings for her and don't want to admit it. I didn't mean for her to figure out that we're brothers or to scare her, I was joking," Reggie said sadly, standing up to take his plate from the table and Hayes' too when he offered it to him.

"Did you see that shit, man? She lives her life in fucking fear! Do you know today was the first time I have ever seen her relax and actually smile since I met her? She's in survival mode all the time, that's all she has. We gotta get her out, Reggie, ASAP. In the meantime, I'm going to do everything I can to get you in that house to protect her full-time." Hayes sighed, standing up to go check on Makia.

"Like I said I'm down for whatever, Hayes, and just so you know, after seeing that shit on top of what he did to her face, prison is the only thing keeping me from killing his ass when I drop her off tonight," Reggie said, taking the dishes to the dishwasher.

———

Makia sat down with her back against the wall in the dark bathroom, tears rolling down her face. She was asking God again what she and her family had done for them to be punished this way. It wasn't until she reacted the way she did on the patio that she realized how deep Michael's impact really was.

Until she was no longer his wife she would always be on guard and high alert ready to fight his ass until she took her last breath. She was tired of it. The gravity of the situation hit differently when she actually let her guard down and tried to be normal like she had done today and it hurt even more. Her parents had knowingly sold her to a monster and so far, there was nothing she could do about it.

A soft knock on the door had her lifting her head from her knees. She watched as Hayes stepped into the bathroom, looking around frantically until he saw her in the corner. Without a word or turning the lights on, he grabbed one of the fluffy, white towels from the towel rack and wet it. She watched while he wrung it out and sat down next to her on the floor and began to wash the now streaked makeup from her face.

"I know you're not okay so I won't ask. Just know that with

me and Reggie's help you will be," Hayes promised, still washing her face.

"I'm sorry, Hayes, for what happened out there but I'm sure you can understand why. I'm also sorry I guessed about Reggie too, but you have to understand after what my parents did and the lengths they took to do it, I spend a lot of time watching the people around me and I really listen when they talk so I just blurted it out. I know you have no more reason to trust me than I have to trust you but I promise I will never say a word to Michael about it. After the way he used my sister and grandmother to control me, I would die before I was the reason he was able to manipulate someone else the same way," Makia said softly, tears still running from her eyes.

"Hey, you have no reason to apologize, okay? The reason I didn't tell you Reggie was my brother is a simple one, plausible deniability. It's easier to argue the truth than it is a lie, if it ever came up. In theory, you would be telling the truth, even though I knew it was a lie, but thank you for keeping it a secret even though it's not my biggest concern. Right now, I need to be able to focus on you and only you so we can handle this situation, cool?" he asked, grabbing another towel and wetting it with cold water this time before laying it on the back of her neck.

"Cool. Do you really think you can help me figure a way out of this?" Makia asked, actually beginning to feel hopeful.

"I know I can, and even if I couldn't, I know people who can. It's just going to take me some time to untie all the legal ropes he has tangled up in this shit but I'm patient enough to handle it. You look tired, when was the last time you got some rest?" He stood up and helped her to her feet.

She rolled her eyes and threw her head back, in a hope to combat more tears. "You already know what happened the last time I tried to sleep in that house, so I've been catching a nap at the studio every day," Makia admitted, scrutinizing herself in the mirror.

She was a mess! Her face was still bruised, her neck too, and it looked worse than when Michael first caused the marks. Her eyes were red and puffy from crying with dark circles underneath them. She could be an extra for *"The Walking Dead",* no makeup required. She dropped her head as new tears began to fall.

"Hey, it's going to work out, I promise. You will be free to do whatever you want soon enough, baby girl," he reassured her, rubbing her back.

"It's not that. I know it's silly but I didn't realize how bad I looked until now. I know it's vain but the stress of all of this is really starting to show," she admitted, lifting her head and looking at him through the reflection in the mirror. He called her baby girl, no one's ever called her that except him. Why did she like it so much? Why did it make her feel so safe?

She watched him bite the inside of his cheek as he stared down at her. "Makia listen to me, you're one of the most beautiful women I have ever met, period. As much as I hate to admit it, Reggie is right. I've been attracted to you since I met you at your parents' house but before I could even act on it, Michael was inviting me to your engagement party. Makia, in another lifetime I would have pursued you to the ends of the earth if I had to, just to make you mine," Hayes admitted, reaching out to touch her hair she had taken down from the French twist she'd worn earlier.

She reached out and touched his hair too, like she had been dying to do all day, smiling sadly up at Hayes. "Good to know and for the record, you would never have had to travel that far to win my heart, Hayes, I would have given it to you freely," she said, moving to walk past him and out of the bathroom.

Makia was going to find Reggie and have him take her

back to the studio. Being this close to Hayes right now was fucking with her rational thought process. Her thoughts on relationships and love were tainted by Michael and all of his BS and how could she even begin to rationalize her and Hayes? It just wasn't a good idea. She loved how she felt when she was around him, especially after this afternoon, and damn she wanted those feelings to last but she was Michael's wife and she respected that, even if he was an abusive asshole.

Hayes walked out of his office an hour later. He was so upset his face felt hot. He thought he knew all that Michael and her parents did to force her into this, but seeing it all in black and white was disgusting. Makia was twenty years old when this all started and was in way over her head and they knew it, and to dangle her love and loyalty to her sister and grandmother the way they did had him seeing red.

After the newest discoveries, Hayes knew he needed to fast forward his time table to sever business ties with Michael and get Makia out of the marriage at the same time so he decided he needed Ryd. He just needed to talk to Makia to make sure she was okay with involving someone else before he moved forward with it. After seeing what they did to her, he vowed to never make another decision on her behalf without consulting her first.

He walked through the house and checked the rooms and patio twice looking for her and was about to call Reggie when he found her sitting in the center of a group of trees off to the side of the backyard opposite of the pool area where there was grass. She was barefoot, her sandals rested in the grass next to her. Her toenails were painted dark purple and he was beginning to think purple, no matter the shade, was her favorite color.

Makia was drawing in her sketchbook with charcoal. Again, he paused to take in the moment as he watched her in her element. Her fingers were black and covered in charcoal, her hands moved effortlessly across the white paper as if they were detached from her body. Her head was down with some of her curly long hair pushed behind her ear while she worked. She had a smile on her face as her drawing took on the look that she wanted it to.

From what he could see it was a self-portrait. In the picture, she had blue streaks in her hair and a hoop nose ring. The camera in the sketch looked like it was fused to her hands and she had a bright and infectious smile.

"So, did you come to find me to talk to me, apologize to me, spy on me, or dare I dream it, kiss me?" Makia asked, smiling at him over her shoulder before he could even utter a word.

"I-u-I came to uh-" Hayes stuttered, his entire train of thought gone, between her smile and what she just said had rendered him stupid.

"I was just messing with you Hayes, damn! I wish you could see your face," Makia laughed putting her charcoal and sketchbook aside patting the blanket Reggie gave her and she had spread out under herself, inviting him to sit.

"So seriously, what's up?" she asked scooting over to make room for him on the blanket.

"Is this what you're really like? I mean when you're not in 'Goku' mode?" he asked, smiling at her while picking up her sketchbook.

"You have got to be kidding me, you watch *"The Office"* and Anime? God really does hate me and has the sickest sense of humor! And yes, this is what I'm like normally." Makia shook her head looking down at her sketch. "What do you think?" she asked curiously.

"That I had no idea you were a photographer too, you

would look good with a nose ring and blue highlights, you have the most beautiful smile I have ever seen and you are very talented," Hayes answered looking from the sketch back to her.

Makia laughed again. "Thank you, I really appreciate that but that's not me, it's my sister Sage, she's two years older than me and a photographer. This sketch is for a special project I'm doing, called 'Home'. I'm painting a portrait of the three of us, me, Sage and my Grandma Lo all doing what makes us the happiest, so Sage with her camera, my grandmother dancing, and me painting, then I want to combine the three together in a fourth portrait. I'm going to hang them in the new house when this is all over. Things have been so bad lately that I hadn't even thought about working on them again, until today," she told him touching the sketch of Sage thoughtfully, smiling down at it.

"Damn, you two could pass for twins, seriously. What inspired you to pick the project back up?" he asked as his finger skated over her charcoal stained ones.

"You did. Well, you and Reggie but still, I actually feel safe and hopeful for the first time in a long time. I told you I have spent most of the last three years not trusting anyone, picking apart what they say, so I know a liar when I see or hear one and either you are on the up and up or you believe with everything inside of you that you are."

"Well, I need to make sure you get to hang those portraits sooner rather than later then. After looking at the contracts I think I do need to bring someone else in, someone I trust even more than Reggie, baby girl," he informed her and touched her hand reassuringly when he felt her body stiffen next to him.

"Who do you want to bring in?" she asked nervously, picking up her charcoal pencil again. "Don't forget Michael seems to know everybody."

Hayes could feel the wall she always had up starting to rise again, she had pulled her knees up and rested her chin on them, the same position she was in the bathroom, she was going back into defense mode.

"My father, Rydwan Purcell," he answered, sliding the pencil from her fingers to look at it closer, it wasn't round. It was four-sided and looked like, well, like a pencil shaped piece of charcoal.

"Rydwan Purcell, I've heard that name before but why?" She turned her head looking over at him curiously.

"He's one of the most sought-after attorneys in the state of Virginia, he's known for his uncanny way of lulling the opposing counsel into a false since of security before gut punching that ass!" Hayes chuckled mimicking the action of a gut punch. "His words not mine, but he's a good guy, you should Google him." He suggested watching her, happy she seemed to be relaxing again.

"I'll do that but why would the most sought-after attorney in Virginia help me? I mean I know he has got to be busy as hell and I'm sure my shit is way too messy to want to even get involved with, I'm surprised you're still here to be honest," Makia said with a mirthless chuckle still resting her head on her knees.

"Ryd is semi-retired now so time will not be an issue but I'm 100% sure he will help us and do it gladly because, like I said, he's a good guy, not to mention I'm his son and he will do anything for his family. And last and certainly not least, he despises Michael Hansen. I think he hates him even more than you do."

Makia sat back up and dusted some of the charcoal from her fingers and smiled.

"I don't think that's even possible but okay let's do it, bring your father in so he can 'gut punch his ass'!" Makia agreed, mimicking the same move that Hayes had to imitate his father.

## Chapter 6

*Present day*

"Hey, what are you doing here, I didn't see your car outside?" Makia asked Sage when she walked into her studio on the second floor, putting her purse and water bottle down.

Because none of the lights were on downstairs and she hadn't seen her car, she thought Sage wasn't there. She was lying on the antique settee lounge Makia had in the corner.

Sage lifted her head, tears rolling down her face, as she looked at Makia. "I needed to talk to you and I didn't want anyone to know I was here," Sage said before covering her face and crying even harder.

Makia quickly rushed to her side and pulled Sage into her arms. "Sage what's wrong? Is it Grandma? Oh my God you said you didn't want anyone to know you were here! Was it Michael? Did he come here? What did he do to you? I will split his ass open if he hurt you!" Makia threatened firing off questions while checking Sage for injuries.

"Sissy! Makia! Calm down, damn! Grandma is okay and

you and I know Michael is too much of a pussy to come here again especially now that the judge upheld the restraining orders me and my client have against him. Did you know he tried to send some people over to bully Spiro to force him to get the restraining order lifted? The man is certifiable, I swear." Sage rambled the way she always did when she was nervous or really upset about something.

"Sage! Yes you told me that remember? Now why the hell are you up in the loft crying your eyes out being all dramatic and shit? This is so not like you at all!" Makia snapped walking across the room and bringing Sage back the box of tissues from her desk.

"Me and Joslyn broke up, she's moving to New York this weekend, her mom lives there now," Sage told Makia, her eyes filling with tears again.

Makia blinked at her in disbelief, they had been together since high school, they were the relationship everyone they knew wanted!

"What? Are you serious Sage? What the hell happened?" Makia asked, sitting next to her again.

"You Sissy, you and Grandma happened. She wanted me to relocate and move to New York and I told her I could never leave you guys," Sage choked out through her tears and ran her hand through her hair. Makia noticed she changed her highlights to pink, it was October so she knew they were temporary for Breast Cancer Month.

"Sage you love her, you are about to get married. I can handle this, go to New York and be happy. You cannot sacrifice your happiness like this," Makia reasoned, wiping away her sister's tears.

"Oh you mean the way you did when you married Michael to save us? I refuse to leave you, 'Kia. I can't leave you here alone with that fucking monster!" Sage sobbed, hugging Makia tight.

Makia moved out of Sage's embrace and grabbed a tissue from the box to wipe her eyes.

"I won't be alone, I still have Grandma and you. You just won't be as close as you are now, that's all. I can always come out there to see you. So what's the big deal?" Makia asked trying to sound and appear calm but inside she was fucking losing her shit, her sister and best friend was leaving her!

"Makia, come on, the only reason this place is still standing and he doesn't come here is because of me and that restraining order and if I'm not here anymore he doesn't have to stay away," Sage said sadly, wiping her eyes. "Besides, Joslyn's been with me forever, she knows what's going on and how much you did and are doing to protect me and Grandma, to even suggest I choose between you guys and her, is just plain heartless on her part."

"Maybe it is, Sage, or maybe she is tired of living her life waiting for the other shoe to drop with Michael. He is like the big bad wolf in all of our lives right now," Makia said trying to see things from Joslyn's point of view.

"If that's the case, then it's a good thing she's going. I want her to live her life to the fullest and be happy even if it's not with me," Sage choked out beginning to cry harder.

Makia squeezed her sister's hands and sighed. "Look, Sage, I want you to think about it, really think about it and if you can save your relationship, save it. If this studio is what's stopping you from leaving don't let it be. This building is just that, a building, an inanimate object. What we do inside this building is what makes it a studio, even without this place you are still one of the best damn photographers on the planet and I'm still an artist, yeah I will miss the refuge this place has provided over the last few years but you mean more to me than some damn building! So if we got to let it go to let you live your life then that is what we gotta do," Makia reasoned looking around her studio before looking back at Sage.

"I will never know what I did to be blessed with a kickass little sister like you but I am grateful every day that I was," Sage said smiling at Makia, impressed with how strong and brave her little sister continued to be in the face of anything.

She looked around at all the paintings Makia created and was in the process of creating and her eyes paused on a sketch and partially painted portrait of that sketch in the center of the room, so Sage knew this was the piece Makia was working on. Now she was 100% gay but the subject of both the sketch and painting had to be the most beautiful man she ever laid eyes on in her life.

"Hey Sissy, who is that?" Sage asked Makia, pointing at the easel.

Makia followed her line of vision and instantly smiled when her eyes landed on the sketch of Hayes, when she noticed Sage watching her with a frown she dropped her gaze.

"Oh, he is one of the models from the gallery I used. I loved how the sketch turned out so I decided to make it a portrait," Makia lied, blushing from her head to her feet.

Sage looked over at the sketch again. The man in the picture was lying in a massive bed on his back, his light brown eyes were sexy and low, she could tell whoever he was focused on was the reason for the provocative closed lip smile on his face. His long dreads were spread out on the pillow behind him, he looked like he was just waking up.

With her photographer's eye, she was trying to discern if he was completely naked or not because of the way Makia had drawn the sheet only across his waist and privates, but she pushed that thought from her head because she knew her sister and there was no way in hell she would be in a naked man's bed while she was still married to Michael. Still she was amazed at how Makia had captured every detail of him from his muscular chest to his long, hair sprinkled legs, she even drew the gauzy curtain in motion above his head perfectly. Sage could almost feel the connection between them.

"Nah, Sissy, try telling that shit to somebody else. I know you and while I know you would never sleep with another man while you're married to Michael, this is a very intimate picture, Sissy, so explain." Sage smirked, folding her arms as she narrowed her eyes at Makia.

Makia sighed staring at the sketch, her heart beat faster as she remembered that day. *It was so hot outside but she went out to sketch in her favorite spot in the trees anyway, she loved the fact that with Reggie as her bodyguard, Michael stopped bugging her so much so she often opted to hang out after her meetings with Hayes to sketch and relax instead of going back to the studio, she loved the peace and quiet.*

*Hayes scared the hell out of her and Reggie by passing out after a few laps in the pool. After the doctor treated him for mild heat stroke, Makia decided to sit with him while he slept in case he woke up and needed anything.*

*She tried to convince herself the act of kindness was just a small way for her to pay him back for all he was doing to help her and had nothing to do with her growing attraction for him.*

*He was laying on his back wearing just his swim trunks, and as he rested he managed to kick his legs out of the sheet covering him.*

*She watched him sleeping for over an hour before deciding to draw him, the minute she grabbed her sketch pad and pencil his eyes opened, seeing the pad and pencil in her hand, he lay still and let her draw him. In her artistic mind his swim trunks muddied her work so she drew him without them.*

Makia blinked remembering that special moment between her and Hayes, her mind slowly brought her back to her messy reality.

"That is Hayes Purcell, he's Michael's business partner and I think I'm in love with him," Makia admitted blushing and looking down at her hands, her eyes filling with tears, not wanting to see the look of disappointment in her sister's face.

Sage quietly stood up and walked over to the sketch picking it up and walking back over to Makia, she put her finger under her chin and lifted her head, making her look at her.

"Why does that make you cry, Sissy? You deserve some happiness too," Sage told her, looking down at the sketch of Hayes. "Does he love you as much as you obviously love him?"

Makia reached out and ran her fingers down Hayes' face in the sketch, causing the charcoal to smear. "Because it's not right, knowing who he is. I shouldn't want to love him let alone be in love with him, and unfortunately no, he doesn't love me back. I mean why would he? I'm just the neurotic mess of a woman married to his asshole partner. So yeah, while I do deserve happiness in life, it is not going to happen with Hayes Purcell."

Sage handed her the sketch and smiled, shaking her head. "You sure about that? This sketch says otherwise, I think you both have it pretty bad too. So stop hanging your head, Makia, nothing that brings you joy should ever bring you shame. And when the time is right and all this Michael mess is behind you, Makia, don't fight it. Love him and let him love you, if there is anyone in this world who deserves it, it's you, Sissy."

Sage looked from the sketch to Makia before hugging her tight again.

"I hear what you're saying, Sage and let's say, for shits and giggles, you're right about him loving me too, I will still be his business partner's ex-wife. I mean how will that look to people? They will think I'm an opportunistic gold digger or something. Even though all of this is wasted conversation because that man does not love me, I know he likes me but that's about it. I mean who can blame him? Most of the time I've been around him I either tried to take his head off at the gym because of his connection to Michael or accused him of being shady." Makia told Sage actually shocked that Sage wasn't reading her the riot act right now for falling for someone in the 'enemy's' camp.

"Girl Bye! This man looks like he is seconds away from jumping your bones. Furthermore, as far as I am concerned and anyone with half a brain for that matter, you ain't married to Michael. You're a damn prisoner of a war with money you should have never been a part of. So forget anyone who might have a problem with you *finally* having some damn happiness in your life when it does happen!" Sage snapped, snatching the sketch away from her. "Besides, do you see how beautiful this man is? Ain't no way in hell I would let anyone tell me I couldn't have him if he wanted me too. Talk about motivation to get this Michael shit figured out sooner rather than later," Sage admonished, looking down at the sketch of Hayes again, her face lit up with a wicked grin.

Makia's eyes widened in surprise. "Sage, what the hell? Need I remind you you are gay, like never been attracted to a guy ever gay!"

"Girl, gay is my sexual orientation, and has nothing to do with my eyes! Being gay doesn't mean I can't appreciate a good-looking man when I see one and way to go, Makia because this one is a freaking work of art!" Sage countered holding up the sketch for Makia to see, as if she needed convincing.

"That he is, Sissy, that he is. He's so much more than that too, he is simply amazing! He is business savvy, and smart. Hayes has such a good heart and just wants to see good happen in the world. The only time I ever see him truly angry is when he has to deal with Michael. I have no idea how he got partnered up with Michael in the first place. He goes out of his way to help in the community and always makes me smile and laugh. He's just, I can't find enough words to describe all the reasons I'm attracted to him. You just have to meet him, do you think you might want to meet him one day?" Makia asked blushing again and her whole face lit up with a smile.

Sage scoffed trying to look serious. "Hell yeah I want to

meet him! I have to know who has my sister drifting on the wings of love and see if he is really worth the trouble, I want to photograph him too," Sage answered thoughtfully looking at Hayes' sketch again.

Makia snatched the sketch back from her sister giving her the evil eye. "Back off, Sissy. I will hurt you!" Makia joked, her smile played with the corner of her mouth for several seconds before she started laughing, seconds later Sage joined in.

"Girl, like I'm sure the artist in you feels like the photographer in me, I just want to capture him, like in dark colors and sterile white backgrounds. He doesn't even seem like he's actually real," Sage reasoned still looking at Hayes' sketch but in an artistic way.

"Oh but he is real, Sissy, really, really real and trust me I get it, the first time I met him was at the parentals' house when you were supposed to meet Michael and even as pissed off as I was, all I wanted was a pencil and a piece of paper to draw him," Makia admitted matter of factly.

"Yeah, well it looks like you want to do more than draw his ass!" Sage teased Makia, laughing.

"Shut up, Sage, and thank you for not making me feel bad about liking him."

"Like I said, Sissy, nothing that brings you joy should ever bring you shame so don't thank me for understanding, thank God for bringing him into your life. After two years of dealing with evil ass, Minute Man Michael and his crazy? You deserve some happiness, Makia."

## *One year and eleven months ago*

"Makia, I'd like you to meet Rydwan Purcell, my father," Hayes said walking her into his father's office three months after they met to go over things at 'Paradise'.

It still made her shake her head and smile that he and Reggie really did call their house 'Paradise', but hanging out there as much as she did lately she understood why.

When Hayes didn't need her to answer questions or go over information she lost herself in the trees and sketched until it was time for her to head back to the city and Michael.

Hayes and his father had been working around the clock to pore over the documents pertaining to her marriage and the ownership of the properties he was using to control her. Once Rydwan had a game plan that Hayes agreed with, he requested a meeting with Makia.

"Nice to meet you, Mr. Purcell," Makia said shyly. Shaking Rydwan's massive hand, she came to realize all the men in Hayes' family were handsome.

Rydwan Purcell was tall and distinguished with a salt and pepper beard with piercing eyes and intimidating demeanor. He was buff and solid, taller than both Reggie and Hayes, although she could see how much Reggie resembled him and where his good looks came from. Even casually dressed and smiling he had such a strong, no nonsense presence about him.

"No Mr. Purcell needed, Makia you can call me Ryd like all of my friends and family do, as much as Hayes talks about you I feel like you are already family. I have to admit seeing you for the first time I can now understand my son's infatuation with you," Ryd said, shooting Hayes a teasing glance and shaking hands with Makia causing her to blush.

"Ryd! Seriously Pops?" Hayes snapped pulling out a chair in front of Ryd's massive mahogany circular table for her to sit in.

Rydwan took note of the action with a smirk. "What? Look at you being all gentlemanly and shit, besides all I was doing was paying her a compliment, she is a beautiful woman and if that embarrasses you, son, then so be it. Now shall we get started?"

Rydwan put on his glasses and sat down at the head of the table and handed a folder to each of them, ignoring Hayes' hostile glare.

Makia was still stuck on stupid from Rydwan's statement about her 'already being family'. She wondered what that was about. Her attraction to Hayes already had her on sensory overload and working so close to him both at the gym and his house had her about to lose her ever loving mind!

So having confirmation that he liked her too was a bit too much to handle right now, it was all so wrong on both of their parts or at least that's what she told herself on a constant loop in her head. She had caught him looking at her more times than she wanted to admit, his eyes moving up her body in such an intimate way that it gave her chills but when he realized she was watching him too, he'd drop his gaze and move away from her.

She also noticed recently that Reggie had begun to sit in on their meetings, she wondered if it was to ease the tension between them.

Needless to say, in the past three months she had been driving herself crazy trying to keep her growing feelings in check when she was around Hayes. Now to hear Rydwan tell it, it appeared he was going just as crazy as she was! God, she hoped so! She had been climbing the freaking walls!

"Makia, I looked over all the documents you gave to Hayes as well as the addendums Hansen tried to get away with at the eleventh hour and I have to say he is a calculated son of bitch and the legal wrangling you have to do to get out of this free and clear looks like it's damn near impossible." Rydwan paused to sip his coffee looking serious and even more intimidating in glasses than he did without them.

"Well hell, I guess that's it then, I have two choices: Stay with Michael until one of us kills the other one or me, Sage and my grandma Lola are just going to have to get used to being penniless and homeless! Cardboard is in, right?" Makia sadly joked with a sigh, her heart caught in her throat as tears sprang to her eyes, feeling hopeless once again.

Rydwan reached over and opened the folder he'd given her before patting her reassuringly on the hand. "Save those tears for another time, like when we gut punch his ass!" Rydwan mimicked a gut punch, making Makia smile and quickly wipe her tears and Hayes drop his head chuckling.

"As I was saying, it would be damn near impossible for the average lawyer. Lucky for you, my son was smart enough to come to me and exploit my love for him and my hatred for your um, what exactly do you call Hansen?" Ryd asked her curiously.

Makia took a deep breath, fighting back a devious smile. "My sister and I call him 'Minute Man'." She blushed looking at both Rydwan and Hayes who were both trying to not to laugh.

"I see. Well, first and foremost, we have to revert the ownership of both the studio and your grandmother's house back to you and your sister, a Miss Sage Sallow. Since you two were the rightful owners of both the minute you turned eighteen years old and your parents had no legal right to sell them to Hansen in the first place," Rydwan informed her, pointing out the first of many documents in the folder he provided her with.

"I'm sorry, what?" Makia asked carefully, quickly reading over the document, she didn't want to get too happy too fast but could it be true?

"You and your sister are the owners of your studio and the

home your grandmother Lola Sallow resides in. Apparently, when your father forced her out of the company, your grandmother still trusted him because he was able to talk her out of most of her assets too, but she left off two and he was so focused on getting his hands on her shares in the company and her money he missed that he became sole owner of all of her assets except for the studio *she*, not your parents, bought you and your sister and her house. I talked to her attorney who got me the original certificates of ownership with her addendum signing both over to you when you were of age." Rydwan instructed her to move to page two in the folder.

"So let me get this straight, if you get the ownership reverted back to me and Sage, Michael doesn't own it, we do?" Makia asked Rydwan, wanting so badly to jump up and dance happily.

"Technically yes, but since you are legally married to Hansen, so does he and with the way your marriage contract is worded, if you leave before the seven years is up, everything you own becomes his, so it's a double-edged sword," Rydwan explained pulling out her original marriage contract.

Hayes stiffened and balled his fist in frustration. "What the fuck! How could your parents do something like this to you? And your father cheated his own fucking mother? Pops, please tell me you have a way to get her out of this without her losing everything sooner rather than later," Hayes pleaded looking at Rydwan, his jaw jumping angrily as he gritted his teeth.

"Trust me, son, you already know I do. Like I said, Hansen is a calculating son of a bitch and sharp as a tack business wise but like your parents he's also greedy and that greed sometimes makes him sloppy. This situation is a tangled mess and has a lot of red tape to sift through but I'm confident I can get through it, all I ask of you, Makia is your patience and your honesty. Sometime in the near future I will have to ask some very personal questions to answer arguments that will arise from Hansen's camp and I will need full disclosure, understand?"

"I understand and I have nothing to hide," Makia told Rydwan before looking over at Hayes who was rubbing his chin looking at her thoughtfully.

"I respect that Makia and let's just say for argument's sake, if that was to change in the future, I still expect the same cooperation and honesty," Rydwan said matter of factly looking over his glasses at her and Hayes in turn with a knowing smirk, just like the one Reggie always had.

"Makia, I forgot to warn you of one of my father's only faults, he has zero, and I mean zero filter," Hayes' explained to her, casting a withering look in his father's direction.

"Ryd, I-I mean Hayes and—" Makia started and was cut off when Rydwan raised his hand, shaking his head with a patient smile.

"No need to say anything else, I just wanted you both to be aware of what I was picking up on and it might be something discussed in great detail in the future. It's been a pleasure to meet you, Makia and I will be in touch as things progress, and I promise you I will have you out of this tangled mess sooner than you think." Rydwan started closing his folder, standing up and smiling over at her.

She noticed he had marked certain documents in the folder with colored sticky notes, they were peeking out all over the place. It made her happy and hopeful that even though he was doing this as a favor to Hayes, he was still taking it seriously.

Slowly she stood up from her own chair, trying to wrap her head around all Rydwan had told her.

"Thank you, Ryd, I really appreciate your time." Makia quickly shook his hand and walked out of his office, closing the door behind her since Hayes was still seated; she assumed he needed to talk to his father privately.

"Sorry about that, I often forget how intense Ryd can be at times, he is very in your face and whatever pops up in his head comes pouring out of his mouth," Hayes explained nervously after ten minutes of tense silence while he drove them back to his and Reggie's house.

Makia was still going over everything Ryd told her in her head but what kept coming back to the forefront of all that information was what he said about her and Hayes. He basically alluded to the fact that he knew she didn't have secrets now but she might in the future and those secrets would involve Hayes. She wasn't stupid and knew exactly what Ryd meant but she kept asking herself, was she out of her rabid ass mind?

Even after a divorce, them being together could possibly cost her everything, if Michael and his heartless lawyers were able to convince a judge they'd had an affair, especially since he was in the process of severing all business ties as well.

"I get it, lawyers are like that sometimes," Makia said quietly staring out of the window, still processing her thoughts and emotions.

Hayes just smiled at her and sighed before returning his attention to his driving, he looked like he was deep in thought too.

They rode in silence and by the time Hayes pulled up in front of 'Paradise' and helped her out of the car before escorting her into the house, she knew they couldn't avoid the conversation they needed to have any longer.

She noticed Regina wasn't in the driveway so she knew Reggie wasn't home so this was the perfect time for them to talk.

"Hungry? I can throw something together right quick," Hayes offered as soon as he closed the door, walking towards the kitchen, while she stood in the living room.

"Hayes, maybe later but right now I think we need to talk, don't you?" Makia reached out and stopped him in his tracks.

He dropped his head and blew out a long breath before turning around to look at her. "Shit, my family is always interfering with my life!" he said with a smile looking down at her shaking his head.

Makia sighed, smiling back at him. "It's only because they want what's best for you, Hayes. They want you to be happy," she said, defending Reggie and Rydwan for spilling his secrets. "And honestly what's going on between us right now? There is no happy ending. Things with Michael are about to get very ugly, and honestly I don't want to drag you even further into this mess especially after what you are already doing to help me."

Hayes stepped closer to Makia, close enough for her soft floral scent to tickle his nose. "Makia, I'm perfectly aware of how ugly things may and probably will get with Michael. And babygirl, I wouldn't do anything to make things worse for you, you have to know that. With that being said when the dust settles you have to know I will stop at nothing to have you. I know you heard what Ryd said and why he said it."

"I heard what he said, but I really want to talk about why he said it, Hayes. We are attracted to each other and let's face it ignoring it just ain't gonna make it go away. And as crazy as it sounds, I have to be honest, I'm not sure if I want it to go away but it has to." Makia blurted out looking deep into Hayes' hypnotizing eyes before taking a step back to put some space between them. She was so nervous to be having this conversation she was shaking all over but it was one they needed to have.

Hayes looked down at her and sighed, shaking his head, begging his hardening body to cooperate so they could have this conversation. Being around Makia lately was like actual torture, he didn't trust himself not to do or say the wrong thing.

This is not what he signed up for when he decided to help her, he thought he could keep it professional but his emotions had other plans and he fell for her, fast.

"For the record, I never intended for this to happen any more than you did, Makia, but regardless of what you or I say, it is happening. But I need you to know that no matter what I'm in your corner. I'm not going anywhere," Hayes stated, reaching out and stroking the curly hair at the back of her neck.

Chills began to radiate through Makia, starting at her shoulders and moving downward. His fingertips kept lightly touching her neck as he played with her hair and with all the pent-up feelings she felt for Hayes her body was super sensitive to his touch.

She closed her eyes for a brief moment to revel in the feelings coursing through her body before opening her eyes and looking into his again. "Okay, I understand and in the meantime I have a request to make," Makia informed him, putting her hands behind her back and interlocking them. Her fingers twitched like they did when she needed to paint but it was because she longed to take his dreads down out of the simple braid running down the back of his head and run her fingers through them.

Hayes continued to stroke the back of her neck, he fought to keep his distance when all he wanted was to press his body against hers and hold her close. "And what's that Makia?"

Makia took a deep breath and several steps back to put some much-needed distance between them. "I need you to not touch me like you just did until my divorce is final. Please don't misunderstand but this is all so confusing and hard enough, you touching me just makes it all that much harder. I also think after today, unless we are meeting with Ryd, I'm going to spend my down time at the studio, not here. We can't leave anything to chance once Michael gets served and let's face it no matter what our intentions are, a few more times alone and we would be into some serious shit we can't come back from," she said moving even further away from him and back over to her portfolio and the folder of information from Rydwan.

Hayes ran his hand down his face and prayed for self-control. He had never wanted a woman the way he wanted Makia but he knew it was much more than lust, he had fallen in love with her and he loved her enough to wait until they could be together the right way.

"That's not even a request you should have had to make, I'm sorry I overstepped my own boundaries just now. I have been trying my best to keep my feelings in check and they had a mind of their own today. Nonetheless, I can assure you it won't happen again. Now back to my original question, are you hungry? Should I throw something together for lunch or do you want to wait for Reggie to get back so he can take you downtown?" he asked folding his arms, smiling down at her, wishing she would change her stance, standing with her arms behind her back caused her breasts to jut forward in the most inviting of ways.

"I could eat, what sounds good to you?" Makia asked sitting in the plush chair by the window opening the folder from Rydwan on her lap.

A muscle in his jaw jumped as he clenched his teeth, flames leapt into his eyes as he looked at her, his thoughts going rogue once again. "Makia, you don't want to know what sounds good to me right about now," he admitted shaking his head and turning towards the kitchen. "I'll call you when lunch is ready."

Makia watched his retreating back for a few seconds before covering her face with her hands shaking her head. "My life, I swear!"

## Present Day

"Good afternoon, Makia. It's good to see you again and I have to say you are breathtaking. You look happier each time we meet," Rydwan said to her as he leaned down and kissed her on the cheek. It had almost been six months since the last time she met with Rydwan, she had spent her birthday at the studio with Sage and her grandmother and as far away from Michael as she could possibly get, he was getting worse every day. She prayed that Rydwan called her to meet with him because he was ready to have Michael served.

"Thank you, Ryd. You never fail to give that ego stroke I need." Makia smiled at him as he sat down at the patio table next to her.

Hayes stepped out carrying a tumbler for Rydwan and a glass of sparkling water with ice for her. She thanked him and dropped her gaze immediately. It had been awhile since she had been to 'Paradise' and she had even stopped going to the kickboxing classes at his gym so seeing him now was throwing her off kilter especially with his dreads down his shoulders.

It wasn't until she caught Rydwan studying her while rubbing his chin that she realized her face must be portraying her thoughts and forced herself to clear her head. She took a long drink of her water and gave herself a mental shake.

Hayes came back to the table with his own glass sitting across from her. He smiled deviously when he saw her eyes skate across his dreads. He'd noticed she seemed to really take notice of him when his dreads were loose and wild and after the torturous last six months of not seeing her, he wanted her to feel a little of the frustration he'd been going through.

"Okay, first and foremost, we are clearing up the last of the red tape on your marriage to Hansen, we will be serving him with your divorce papers on the same day of the board meeting, he also has several lawsuits pending including one for sexual harassment filed by his previous personal assistant who is four months pregnant. He will be getting hit on all sides all at once and my concern is, of course, for you and your safety when this all comes down," Rydwan stated looking at Makia with concern.

"I get that. If I know ahead of time, I will make sure to make arrangements to lay low, maybe go to my grandmother's house, Reggie will still be with me, right?" Makia asked, trying not to sound anxious and afraid.

Hayes cleared his throat and sat up straighter in his chair. "Yes, he will make it a point to stay even closer to you leading up to this and the day this all goes down. You know you are more than welcome to stay here," he offered, looking a little concerned himself.

"That brings me to my other point, remember that talk we had about disclosure? Now comes the time for me to ask if you two are in a relationship? If so, when did it start, is it physical?" Rydwan asked, looking at each of them in turn.

Hayes saw Makia blush and look down at her hands before looking his father directly in the eyes. "Ryd, you called it the first day you met her, I do have feelings for Makia, very strong feelings but no, we are not in a relationship nor have we been in the past. As a matter of fact this is my first time seeing Makia after our initial meeting in your office, we both thought it was best to keep our distance from each other until the dust settled," he stated looking over at Makia in a loving way, who had turned her head and was smiling back at him.

"Is this all true, Makia?" Ryd asked with a sigh before scribbling down a few notes and looking at her again.

Makia looked from Hayes to Rydwan before nodding. "Yes, I even stopped taking classes at Hayes and Reggie's gym and went back to my old one just to be on the safe side. All of our communication with each other comes through Reggie too. I didn't want to leave anything to chance for Michael and his vipers to find," she answered.

Rydwan studied her again, rolling his pen around with his fingertips. "I see. You do realize how dangerous this relationship will be for you even after your divorce, correct? Hansen is a sore loser and he plays dirty, remember that. I need you both to promise me to continue to be very careful, understand?" Rydwan asked, looking at them both again.

"I understand, I have a question though, with me only taking what is rightfully mine in the first place will there be a divorce proceeding or will Michael just have to sign the divorce papers?" Makia asked, drinking all of her water, her heart now in the pit of her stomach with fear. Hayes immediately rose grabbing her glass to refill it.

Rydwan watched with amused interest before answering her. "Since you are not interested in anything but what is rightfully yours, namely the property and your trust, he would just have to sign. Be warned though, I have the suspicion he will try to drag this out and drag you through the mud which is why he is being bombarded with everything at once. He will be scrambling to save face and will need all of this messy business to go away quietly and if he still resists I have the signed statement from his previous assistant and the DNA test results from the amniocentesis proving he's the father of her child thus proving his infidelity, not to mention the detailed catalogs of the results of his abuse to you."

Makia accepted her refilled glass from Hayes before looking over at Rydwan with a confused frown. "Documentation of my abuse? What do you mean?" she asked, looking from Rydwan to Hayes.

Hayes took a sip of his water before answering her. "Me. I took pictures of your injuries when you weren't paying attention and gave them to Ryd. From the first time you came to the gym to the last time he hit you. Please don't be upset with me. I just hated what he was doing to you and wanted to make sure he didn't get away with it," Hayes explained looking at her with pleading eyes.

Makia wanted to be mad but she understood why he did it, proof with pictures would go longer than just her word if needed

"Thank you but when did you have time to take pictures of me? I never remember you even doing it," Makia asked Hayes taking the pictures that Rydwan was offering her.

"The gym. I have cameras all over the gym and two in my office," Hayes admitted with a sheepish grin hoping she wasn't too upset, he couldn't tell.

Makia flipped through the pictures and covered her mouth with her hand and began to cry. "It's like looking at a different person, I never realized this was how the rest of the world was seeing me," she said looking at them both before wiping her tears.

"Never again, Makia. You are on short time now, besides if he tries anything it will take an act of God to get Reggie off his ass or myself for that matter. If he lays a finger on you, I'm coming for his fucking head," Hayes vowed reaching across the table to take her hand.

"Okay that being said, I will let you know the exact date he is being served. Until then be safe and stay alert, I don't trust his grimy ass. If he starts acting different in any way let me know," Rydwan instructed and reached over to take her other hand. "And welcome to the family, Makia," he teased casting a withering look at Hayes before standing to leave.

Makia opened and closed her mouth like a fish out of water to find the words to protest but seeing the predatory stare Hayes was casting her way, she knew Rydwan was right. Once her divorce was final she didn't see herself being single too long if Hayes had anything to do with it.

## Chapter 7

"So just remember I need to be there by three tomorrow so we will have to burn rubber from George Mason after class," Makia informed Reggie as he escorted her into her house two nights later.

Just as Hayes promised Reggie was never far away, he even had a room on the first floor down the hall from the kitchen. Unbeknownst to Michael, Reggie had installed microphones throughout the house in case he tried to go after Makia after Reggie retired to his room for the night.

So far so good, since she had not suffered so much as a broken nail since Reggie had been there and now knowing this entire sham of a marriage was coming to an end, Makia was walking on sunshine.

"Okay so I will map it tonight and again in the morning in real time, anything else bef-" Reggie stopped mid-sentence when he noticed Michael standing in the doorway of the dining room, drinking from a highball glass watching them intently.

"Good Evening, Mr. Hansen, it's been a while, I take it

things are well?" Reggie asked walking over with his hand extended to Michael.

Makia immediately noticed Michael's almost unkempt appearance, it reminded her of her father's, the day she found out he and her mother were planning to marry Sage off. Shit! Something was up!

"I'm well, Reggie, I take it all went well today? According to your report, there was a bit of an altercation at the center today?" Michael asked, shaking Reggie's hand but staring at Makia, she noticed his eyes narrowed for a split second.

Reggie's face was impartial, his true feelings never shining through. "I'm not sure what report you're referring to Mr. Hansen, especially since today is Wednesday and Makia teaches the kids at the center on Thursdays," Reggie answered, passing Michael his cellphone with Makia's daily schedule pulled up.

Michael took the phone and after studying the schedule, nodded and passed it back to Reggie. "My mistake," he said annoyed that he was unable to trip Reggie up. He knew Makia was up to something. "Anyway Makia, I thought we would have a light late dinner, it's been ages since I made it home this early and I want to spend some time with my beautiful wife," Michael stated, walking over to her and lightly running his thumb down her cheek. It took all the strength in her body not to slap his hand away, like always, even his light touch made her want to vomit.

"That sounds fine, Michael, why don't you go ahead and tell the cook to serve, I will be there in a few minutes. I have a full schedule tomorrow and need to go over a few details with Reggie before he turns in for the night," Makia answered with a forced smile, yeah his grimy ass was up to something she could tell by how nice he was being to her.

"Sure, but make it quick, I would hate for your dinner to

get cold," Michael warned, his eyes bore into hers before he turned and walked away.

She and Reggie waited until they heard the dining room doors slide closed before speaking.

"Like I was saying, I will map things tonight and double check them in the morning, I will do my best to make sure you get to each appointment on time," Reggie stated then mouthed the words, "Hand me your phone." Makia handed him her phone and he pressed a few buttons before returning it.

"Okay sounds good. Oh yeah, one last thing, I want to add a trip to the gym to my schedule. It's been a few days and I need to tone up," Makia answered out loud then mouthed the words, "Touch base with Ryd and Hayes! He is up to something," to Reggie trying not to panic.

Reggie nodded and moved to go down the hall towards his room, "According to the schedule you sent you have two hours in between the center and the portrait consultation at city hall, I'll add it in there?" Reggie suggested, standing further down the hall but still close enough for her to read his lips, "Don't worry, I can tap in and hear everything from your phone and you know I will."

"Perfect, see you in the morning, Reggie. Sleep well." Makia moved to the dining room doors and slid her phone into her pocket as she went.

She stepped into the dining room not surprised to see Michael still standing by the door when she walked in. Obviously eavesdropping on her and Reggie's conversation.

"I see you and Reggie are getting along well, I have to say I'm surprised by your change of heart," Michael stated following her to the table.

Makia sighed and took her place at the other end of the table, as far as possible from Michael. "Please don't let me being pleasant to Reggie fool you, I still think all of this is a dumb idea but if that is what it takes so you are not blowing my phone up all day I'm with it. Now what is this all about, Michael? As you heard me telling Reggie I have a pretty full day tomorrow and I would like to get some rest."

Michael's eyes landed on the curvy, well-endowed young woman not too much older than Makia as she entered the room carrying their food.

Makia literally had to swallow back the knowing laugh, he had hired another 'cook', seriously how stupid did he think she really was? He would be screwing her within a week if he wasn't already! It wasn't like she cared but this young lady was their third cook in the last six months and she was pretty and young like all the others, hopefully this one could cook.

The cook smiled down at Makia as she placed a plate of food in front of her before returning to the kitchen. The smell that rose from the plate actually made her gag behind her napkin.

"Well, first of all, I wanted to introduce our new cook, Nessa. I thought I'd have her whip something up for us tonight and secondly, I wanted to tell you we are leaving town for the long weekend, spending some quality time together and giving you a break from the security detail," Michael informed her, taking a bite of food and quickly bringing his napkin to his mouth to spit the food into.

"I see. I can tell from your reaction she must be one of the greats and I need more than a day's notice to leave town, Michael. Like I do every weekend, I have plans with my family and since it's a long weekend, we are taking Grandma Lola to the beach, she is finally out of her wheelchair," Makia informed him, taking a small sip of sparkling water.

He must be out of his rabid ass mind if he thought she would ever trust him to go anywhere out of town with him. After coming to blows on their honeymoon, she promised herself, never again.

"It's not a request Makia, we fly out tomorrow night at 7

p.m., so be packed and at the airport by then," he snapped standing up to make himself another drink.

Makia pushed the foul-smelling plate away dropping her napkin on top of it and sat back in her chair. "No, *you* fly out at 7 p.m. tomorrow night and why don't we cut the BS and you just tell me what this is all about so I can go to bed?" she asked calmly, crossing her legs and turning sideways in her chair.

Michael tossed his drink to the back of his throat and winced at the burn as the alcohol slid down his throat. "Makia believe me, now is not the time to fuck with me. You need to have your ass on that plane at seven tomorrow night or your sister and grandmother are done, you feel me?" he threatened glaring over at her, strolling in her direction.

Makia's eyebrow arched but she said nothing, after her last meeting with Ryd she knew she was on short time. Ryd had uncovered Michael had been stealing from his own company and defrauding the investors which was why instead of sepa-rating from Hansen, Hayes was going to call a meeting and have Michael voted out.

So she wondered if this impromptu trip was to get her out of town because he found out about the sexual harassment lawsuit or caught wind that his dirty deeds were catching up with him.

"I'm not going Michael, not today or ever. You must be out of your mind to even suggest I go anywhere with you. I don't trust you and to be honest I don't even like you! I have two jobs and a life, Michael and just because you can flit around hither and yon, Mr. CEO, doesn't mean we all have the same luxu-ries. So unless you want to tell me what the hell is going on, I'm going to take a shower and go to bed because the smell of this food and this entire encounter is giving me a headache," Makia snapped, rising from the table.

Michael was in front of her in an instant. "Have you lost your fucking mind? Did you forget the power I have at my disposal and what it could mean to you and your precious family?! With a phone call, I can make Sage and Granny's ass disappear, they live in *my* shit remember? Oh and these jobs of yours? You might want to go ahead and give notice, because this trip? Is a baby making trip, I've waited long enough and I will have my son, Makia," he growled closing his hand around her throat.

Makia dug her nails in his wrist and pulled his hand away from her throat, throwing it to the side aggressively. This man was a fucking idiot! She knew he hoped an announcement of her pregnancy would give him more clout and drive home the point they really were a happily married couple and dull the light on the bad publicity coming his way. He better pray that his former assistant gives him a son and leave her the hell alone! Who the hell did he think she was, Catherine of Aragon or Anne Boleyn? Boy Bye! The thought of him even touching her once had her retching, there was no way in hell she was giving him an entire weekend!

"Michael, why don't you do it, make that phone call and sell the properties then? You and I both know you won't, don't we? Because that studio and my grandmother's house is the only leverage you have to lord over me and keep me tethered to you and we both know it! You won Michael, enjoy your spoils of war and leave me the hell alone! As for this baby making trip? I would rather *die* before I would purposely bring an innocent soul into this fucked up situation! Besides since your dirty dick ass burned me, according to my doctor I have some severe tubal scarring so that kinda takes me off the baby making market.

"Like I said before, it's gonna be a no from me, dog, and last thing, Michael, this is my final warning. Do. Not. Put. Your. Hands. On. Me. *Ever. Again.* Because if you do, I'm coming at you with all the pent-up frustration and aggression I have had inside of me since the day I met you. I've come to realize I ain't got shit to lose. I have let you bully and manipulate me since I was twenty years old and I'm done. I've accepted my fate and conceded to your victories, this marriage, and even gave up the opportunities I was offered in New York to come back here to get married.

"I've dealt with the security detail and even the monthly fucking lunches where you parade me around the office like a freaking show piece but I am not giving up either one of my jobs. And I will not ever agree to a baby, especially knowing that baby would be used as another way to manipulate me if I can even have one anyway." Makia stood waiting for Michael to make his next move, his jaw worked angrily as he held his wrist in his hand, she had broken the skin with her nails. The way he was looking at her, she could tell he was taking her apart in his head.

"Good night, Makia, I will cancel the trip but we will be revisiting the baby discussion, just not tonight. I can see it would be counterproductive in your current state of mind," Michael snapped, walking back over to the bar to fix himself another drink.

"Good night Michael, and we can discuss it until one of us is blue in the face and my answer will never change, trust fund or no trust fund," Makia informed him, smiling sweetly as the color drained from his face.

"Hold up, why would you bring up your trust fund when all I was talking about is having a baby?" he asked her, now trying to play it cool, his rapid blinking told her he was in panic mode knowing he was busted in another one of his dirty deeds.

"You know something I will never understand about powerful men like you and my father? While astute, brilliant in business, well-liked in most circles, you just can't help bragging to make yourselves look good, unfortunately sometimes the wrong person is listening, like really listening to all the crap you've been talking about just in case they need to use it against you one day." Makia looked at him pointedly before leaving the dining room.

She heard him slam his glass down and follow her out. "Makia, come back here, this conversation is not finished. Now, if your spineless father has told you something about me and my business and your trust, you better tell me now!" he demanded snatching her around to face him by her arm.

Before she could snatch it away and knock him on his ass for touching her again, Reggie was walking into the foyer where they were standing. "Everything all right? How was dinner?" he asked them both smiling a hauntingly evil smile that failed to reach his eyes.

Michael puffed up, glaring at Reggie. "Dinner was fine, just fine, I'm having a private conversation with *my wife*," he snapped in Reggie's direction sizing him up like he was going to fight him.

Reggie chuckled and gave Michael a glance that let him know he did not want those problems before looking over at Makia, who nodded to let him know she was okay.

"Well I respect that, Mr. Hansen but your conversation failed to be private the minute you started yelling in the foyer. Now wasn't it you who instructed me to never let Makia or even myself do anything that would make you look bad?" Reggie asked him, still smiling but in a more concentrated way than before.

"Yes, and what's your point?" Michael snapped, nostrils flaring.

"My point is I'm sure you hold yourself to the same standard and after making myself a sandwich and meeting the new cook, who I might add has been snapping selfies and snapchatting since she served you dinner, you wouldn't want to give her the wrong impression on her first night, would you? Maybe you two can pick this up tomorrow, in the morning, when clearer heads will prevail," Reggie suggested to Michael, dropping his smile. Makia noticed he was now positioned between herself and Michael in a way that if you weren't looking for it, it wasn't noticed.

Michael glared at Makia nodding. "Perhaps you're right, Reggie but let this be the first and last time you ever attempt to correct my behavior or tell me what to do in my own damn house, especially with my wife. Do it again and your ass is fired, play your position young'un, play your position," Michael warned before throwing another crusty look her way and storming back into the dining room.

Makia mouthed the words, 'Thank you' before making her way to her bedroom.

---

*July 1st, 10 a.m.'* was all the text from Ryd said. She almost screamed out loud, she had an exit date! Three weeks had passed since her dinner with Michael and every day he seemed more and more agitated. She was nervous he knew or at least suspected something but with Reggie around she was never alone with him. Her nightmare was finally over!

She put down her paintbrush and sent a message to her grandmother knowing she would be staying at her house starting on June 30th. She knew she would be safer there than at the studio, especially with Reggie there. She was going to have Sage steer clear for a few days too.

"Hey Kia, something popped off at the gym and Hayes can't leave the office so I'm going to run by and check on everything, cool?" Reggie asked her about two hours later, after tapping her on the shoulder to get her attention because she had her music playing in her Air Pods and was in her zone.

"Okay, I hope nothing too bad is going on over there and take your time. I'm not heading back to the house until late because I can go straight to bed instead of verbal sparring with

Michael since he hasn't been around that much lately." Makia smiled at him, rinsing out her paint brush.

Makia was of the mind that after their last talk, Michael was actually tired of fighting her on everything and decided to leave her the hell alone for a while and hopefully she would be out of the house by the time he circled his attention back again.

Reggie nodded thoughtfully. "I feel you, have you noticed he's coming in later and later? I think the last time he beat you home was the night the new cook started, wonder what that's about?"

Makia shrugged and went back to her work. "Who knows and who cares? July 1st is right around the corner and I can leave that Godforsaken house for good or at least begin to."

"For sure, just let me know when and I can move some of your stuff to Paradise," Reggie teased her stepping out of her studio and back into the hallway with a smirk.

"Paradise? Please, I am moving to Grandma Lola's until I find a spot!" Makia told Reggie looking at him like he was crazy.

"Yeah okay," Reggie said with a smirk and knocked on the door frame. "Anyway I'll be back in a few, hit me up if you need something before I get back," Reggie told her before disappearing down the stairs.

Makia pushed her earbud back in and went back to painting. Excitement that she was days away from being free from this nightmare had her smiling again, that and the beautiful man that she was painting staring at her with his deep soulful eyes from the canvas.

Once she was divorced they could start planning their future. Hayes told her several times he didn't mind waiting to get married if that was what she wanted especially after such a bad marriage with Michael.

Her argument was always the same, if they got married or

not, she would be spending the rest of her life with him. She stopped painting and stared at the portrait of Hayes, to the naked eye it looked fine but to her she needed to get the eyes just right so when someone's eyes met his in the portrait, they felt the love she felt when he looked at her that way.

Her mind was wandering back to Hayes and her need to see him when the alarm app on her phone alerted her that the studio door was unlocked.

Makia put down her paintbrush and moved to go downstairs to lock up when she remembered Sage had a session with a local rock band coming in soon and would probably be there by the time she made it back upstairs and got back into her zone so there was no point. She picked up a different paintbrush and let the love songs playing in her ears and thoughts of Hayes take her back to her happy place.

The crash and immediate pain on the side of her head came out of nowhere, it immediately wrecked her peace and had her seeing stars. She ducked down and turned to see who the hell just hit her.

Michael was standing over her with his fists balled, nostrils flaring like a raging bull, spittle gathered in the corners of his mouth, his chest heaving up and down angrily.

"*You sneaky fucking bitch!*" he roared as he picked her up and threw her across the room, her back cracked against the wall, she felt numb all over. Numb and angry.

Makia staggered to her feet and wiped the blood from her eyes that was running from her head. When he charged again she swung and tagged him in his right eye, smelling the alcohol on his breath.

"You just thought I would let your ass go without a fight? I will kill you before I let that shit happen, do you hear me?" he shouted as he swung when she ducked he tripped her knocking her off her feet. "You will die before I let you leave me!" he roared, the realization of what was happening chilled her to her core. He must have found out about the divorce before they meant for him to.

He kicked her repeatedly until she could no longer move, then picked her up and tossed her across the room again.

Too weak to think straight or fight back, she closed her eyes as his fist smashed down into her face, breaking her jaw, and prayed for Reggie or Sage to come, for Hayes to take her away from the pain like he promised.

It seemed like forever had passed and Michael continued to hit her relentlessly with no sign of stopping, as she moved further and further away from consciousness, she accepted her fate and asked God to protect the ones she loved and even though she didn't want to go, she asked Him to take her home.

---

He paced back and forth in the waiting room like a caged animal waiting for someone to tell him something, anything, about Makia. The nurse had one more goddamn time to ask who he was or tell him she couldn't tell him anything because he wasn't family before he lost his shit!

All he heard in his head was Reggie sobbing, apologizing for leaving her alone on a constant loop in his head, and the paramedics screaming in the background, calling Makia's name asking could she hear them, then one of them saying they finally found a pulse.

The wind was knocked out of his body when the door at the other end of the wing he was pacing in opened and he saw what he thought was Makia rushing down the hall in their direction, he rushed towards her about to take her into his arms when he noticed the blue highlights and nose ring.

"Sage?" he asked reaching out to stop her purposeful gait.

Sage stopped and looked up at him, tears trailing down her face. "Hayes?" she asked while studying his face, even in a panic the photographer in her was cataloging his face. "Do you know anything? Where is she? What happened to her? What did that cowardly son of a bitch do to my sister?" she screamed crumbling against Hayes, who caught her before she could hit the ground.

"I don't know they won't release any information to me. My brother called me and told me the studio was ransacked and he found her in a bloody mess in the corner of her studio," Hayes informed her, helping her to a seat.

"Sage, I'm so fucking sorry! I told her, I promised her that he would never hurt her again. This is all my fucking fault, my fucking fault!" Hayes choked out shaking his head.

Sage sat up and looked at him confused. "Michael is a fucking lunatic! He is the one who did this, why are you blaming yourself, Hayes?" Sage asked, trying to understand his guilt.

"It's my fault Reggie left her alone, my fault! Apparently Michael got wind of what was about to go down and set up an emergency meeting at the office so I couldn't leave when I got the call about a disturbance at the gym. So naturally I called Reggie to go check and he wasn't there when Michael attacked her. Someone in my father's camp took a bribe and Ryd is already combing the servers and collecting everyone's work cellphones to find out who and that person or persons will be dealt with swiftly, I promise you that," Hayes spat angrily, wiping away his tears.

Sage looked at him like he was crazy. "Okay hold up, Reggie? What does Makia's driver have to do with you? What the hell are you even talking about?" Sage asked, looking confused and mutinous at the same time.

If this bastard had been playing with her sister's heart all this time, Michael just got a temporary pardon and Hayes was about to be taking his last breath!

Hayes frowned back at her just as confused. "So are you

telling me Makia never told you Reggie is my brother? That my father Rydwan was helping her untangle this entire mess of a marriage or even that he got the ownership of your properties reversed back to you and her?"

Sage shook her head looking even more confused. "I have no idea what you're talking about," she admitted shrugging her shoulders.

"But she told you about me?" Hayes asked remembering she called him by his name when he called her name.

"I kind of dragged that out of her but yeah she told me about you. By the way, watch your back, Michael smashed a lot of her work but yours was the only one he ripped to shreds so he will be coming for you at some point."

Hayes' entire body stiffened. "I welcome it, if anything is seriously wrong with your sister I am killing his ass," he spat and looked over his shoulder as the nurse he spoke to before came out of the locked double doors and he quickly stood to his feet and rushed over.

"Sir, as I told you before, as you are not family I cannot release any information regarding Mrs. Hansen to you," the nurse informed Hayes holding her hands out to stop him from coming any further.

Sage moved in front of him. "He is family, now tell us what the hell is going on with my sister!" Sage hissed glaring at the nurse.

"Oh ma'am, I am sorry. I didn't realize and who are you to the victim?" the nurse asked, turning red and shrinking under Sage's glare.

"Lady, you got about five seconds before I lose my shit. Now tell me what is going on with my *sister!*" Sage raged, getting loud before breaking down in a fit of tears against Hayes.

"My apologies, I am so sorry Miss… um?" the nurse paused waiting for Sage to give her name.

Hayes threw his head back and swore at the ceiling., "Okay that's it, please get us someone who can provide us information about Makia Hansen," Hayes commanded looking lethal.

The nurse stared at them for a moment longer before nodding and silently moving back through the double doors and turned right back around to follow the dark-haired woman with the messy bun back over to them.

"Are you the family of Makia Hansen?" she asked as she approached them. Hayes quickly read her name tag and realized she was a doctor, he threw the nurse a look that basically asked her why she was still even there. She rolled her eyes and looked at the doctor stubbornly staying in place.

"Yes, I am her sister, now please before I lose the rest of what's left of my mind, tell me what is wrong with my sister," Sage informed the doctor and like Hayes glared at the not so helpful nurse.

"As you know your sister was assaulted and she came in in pretty bad shape, her jaw and both eye sockets are broken, as well as her nose, somehow she has retained all of her teeth. She has five broken ribs, we found several chips in her vertebrae and her right hand is shattered. There is significant brain swelling as well as internal injuries, including damage to her kidneys and stomach. She is out of surgery and in a medically induced coma, we are optimistic she will recover in due time," the doctor informed them in hushed tones and a business-like manner.

Hayes stared straight ahead, his jaw jumped angrily as he held Sage who was sobbing again in his arms. When he got his hands on Michael it was a fucking wrap, his bitch ass was going to die tonight!

"Oh my God, no! Can we see her? Will she be okay?" Sage asked hiccupping through her tears.

"We are optimistic but as I said she has some internal injuries and some of her injuries are very severe. There is no internal bleeding but we cannot say that will remain the case. We worked very hard to get her stabilized after surgery, her heart rate dropped several times. We will continue to monitor her through the night and I would normally advise against it but I will allow you to visit with her, fifteen minutes. If you follow me I can show you to her room," the doctor said, and unlocked the double doors.

Sage was right on her heels, Hayes stayed planted, watching the young unhelpful nurse who quickly looked around before pulling her phone out of her pocket and bringing it to her ear.

Sizing her up, she was most definitely Michael's type, built like an Instagram model, young, and dumb.

He walked over to her and snatched the phone from her hand, holding the handset to his ear, he heard Michael's voice. "She's still alive?" Michael snapped loudly.

"Your ass is mine, bitch!" he hissed, snapped the phone in half and snatched the nurse up by the arm and dragged her into the stairwell. "Did you see what he did to her? Did you fucking see her when they rushed her in here and you have the nerve to call his ass to tell him any fucking thing about her? He tried to kill her and she is his fucking wife! What the hell do you think he will do with a little tramp like you when he's done with you, huh?" Hayes asked the nurse, shaking her by the arm.

"If you don't let me go I will scream!" she threatened turning red again.

Hayes pushed his face close to hers. "Do I look like I give two fucks if you do? Leave. You don't work here anymore, especially after I tell the doctor how I overheard you discussing an assault victim's medical records over the phone. HIPAA, bitch," he growled in her face.

The nurse shook all over and began to cry. "No, no please I need this job, my son, he has cerebral palsy. Michael proposed to me and promised he would pay off all of his medical bills once we got married. I'm so sorry I had no idea he was the one who did that to her! I can tell you where he is, I can help you in any way you need! I promise! Please, please don't tell anyone, I'm begging you!" she sobbed, grabbing hold of the front of Hayes' shirt. He noticed the cheap ass diamond chip set in 10 karat gold on her left hand, shaking his head. Michael was worth over a billion dollars easy and he couldn't even buy the girl a decent ring to pawn when he left her ass alone?

"Save it, your tears don't mean shit to me, you probably don't even have a son," he spat looking her up and down with disgust. "You really want to help me? You let that slimy bastard know I'm coming for his ass and I'm bringing the hounds of Hell with me."

The nurse nodded slowly, tears still running from her eyes. "I'm sorry, he promised to help me with my son and he told me how hateful and mean she was to him and that her boyfriend beat her up. He told me he needed more information so he could divorce her without having to pay alimony. I would never be with an abuser, my mom was beaten to death by my step-dad," she quickly explained looking down at her feet shamefully.

Hayes pulled out his money clip and counted off eight one-hundred-dollar bills. "Here, this is for breaking your phone and if I find out you're lying about your son? I'm coming back. Michael ain't the only one with pockets deep enough to make shit happen and a word to the wise, men like Michael never leave their wives, they just fuck you and promise you the world until they get bored or you get tired of the lies, either way they move on to the next one like you never existed," he snapped and opened up the stairwell door, he nudged her towards the double doors so she could take him to Makia's room.

"Sissy, you have to get better please, Grandma Lola and I love you so much. It can't end like this 'Kia, it just can't."

He heard Sage softly talking to Makia when he walked in, she was sitting next to the bed clutching Makia's good hand, tears rolling in a steady stream down her face as she looked up at him.

"Hayes is here, Sissy. I told you I wanted to meet him and now that we met you gotta come out of this, so we can celebrate your divorce. You hear me, Sissy? You are going to be free from the Minute Man! You and Hayes can be together. Please come back to us, please fight," Sage sobbed dropping her head on the bed next to Makia's hand, her shoulders shook as she cried.

The machines beeped and clicked, all doing their job to help keep Makia alive. Every minute he stood there smelling that sterile hospital smell he kept having to remind himself this was not a nightmare and was actually happening.

Hayes moved closer to Sage and rested a reassuring hand on her back, when his eyes drifted to Makia and he took in all of her visible injuries and the tubes going in and out of her body, he felt physically sick, his knees buckled and he came down next to Sage placing his hand over both of theirs.

"Makia, baby girl, please forgive me. I let you down and it will never happen again I promise you it won't. Please, please, please don't stop fighting, Beautiful, we need you here! We need you here!" he choked out as tears rolled down his face.

Sage lifted her head and looked at him, her eyes red and puffy. "Please tell me you know where he is, we can't let him get away with this," Sage stated looking murderous.

"I've got a few ideas and I called my father, Ryd before you got here, he's got some eyes looking out for him and while we all know this was his doing, we have no proof. They were alone at the studio and I'm sure he has paid off a few people to lie about his whereabouts," Hayes informed Sage biting the inside of his cheek thoughtfully.

"The fuck we don't! I had security cameras installed at the

studio after his stupid ass came up there acting a damn fool the last time! You know, in case he violated the restraining order again," Sage told him, pulling her phone out of her back pocket and logging onto the security app in the studio. Clear as day, you saw Michael enter the studio and rush up the stairs towards Makia's studio.

"Is there a camera up there by chance?" he asked his face hot, hands shaking with rage just seeing him on the feed.

Sage nodded and reached over bringing up the second-floor cameras, her bottom lip trembled as she watched Michael pick Makia up and toss her across the room like trash.

Hayes felt his face grow hot in anger, his thoughts even more lethal than they were a second ago.

"I need you to email these to me, can you do that?" he asked his face set in rage as he shook all over and stood up. "And restraining order? He had a restraining order against him?"

"Yeah, he tried to attack me a few years back and a client of mine was there too. We both have one against the crazy bastard and I'll send you the video footage but what good does this do us if he skips town or the country like the coward he is?" Sage asked taking his business card to send him the videos to his email.

"That shit ain't happening, better still, send those to my phone," he rattled off his number before dialing Rydwan's number.

"Sage, I know the doctor said fifteen minutes but stall her if you can, I'm arranging for security to guard her in case that bastard shows up here and when I get back we need to talk," Hayes ordered rushing from the room, talking to Rydwan as he went.

## *One week later*

He watched through his tears as Sage held the pen and clipboard in her hands, she would press the pen to the paper and break down sobbing, looking over at Makia.

They were told there was nothing more that could be done for Makia, she fell into a deep coma and the only thing keeping her alive at this point were the machines. Being her power of attorney, it was up to Sage to give them permission to turn the machines off. They both agreed Makia would not want to live her last days on earth bedridden in a coma.

The last week had been Hayes' equivalency of Hell. When the news of Makia's assault came out, Michael was voted out by the board, all of his assets and accounts were frozen, ownership of the properties were back in Sage and Makia's hands completely, and in addition to the paternity suit and sexual assault charges he was facing, there was now a warrant for his arrest for assaulting Makia.

Rydwan was pushing for attempted murder and once Makia took her last breath, he would be wanted for murder. Every day he didn't get the chance to exact his own revenge on Michael was another day Hayes descended deeper and deeper into a very dark and violent place. He spent hours at the gym, working the heavy bag the way Makia did when she was at her most frustrated with her marriage to Michael. All he knew was Michael better pray to God the police found him first because he, Reggie, and his PI were looking for him, ready to beat his ass on sight!

Sage took another deep breath looking over at him, he nodded and dropped his head. She closed her eyes and signed the papers before dropping down to her knees and grabbing Makia's hand. "I love you, Sissy, I'm so sorry this is the way God chose to set you free from all of this. I promise you he will pay for what he did to you! I will make him pay," Sage sobbed dropping her head on the bed.

In surreal slowness, Hayes watched them turn off the machines and disconnect all the tubes and IVs. It took everything in him not to tell them to stop. He moved to the other side of her bed and leaned down kissing her on the forehead, tears still running down his face. "You're free baby girl, take care of yourself and promise me you will be standing at the gates of Heaven to greet me when I get there. You were and will always be my first love," Hayes whispered through his tears, his voice cracking as he spoke.

Sage was watching him, as he lovingly touched Makia's face and hair before running his finger down her arm, stopping at the cast on her right hand. He tried to memorize everything about her so he would never forget even the small things that made her so uniquely her.

"Thank you for loving her like you do and all you did to help her," Sage told him, reaching across Makia's bed to take his hand and together, they waited for the woman they loved most in the world to take her last breath.

## Chapter 8

*Two weeks later*

Hayes and Reggie walked down the hill to the beach silently, both clutching white roses in their hands as they walked up to the small group gathered at the edge of the ocean's waves.

Sage looked over as they approached, smiling weakly. It still rocked him to his soul how much she and Makia favored each other. So many times in the last two weeks, he almost grabbed her to him thanking God this was all just a nightmare.

He missed Makia so much it was hard to breathe or even think about going through another day without her. To ease his pain a bit, Sage had given him Makia's self portrait of the 'Home' series she was working on for their new house.

He fell asleep staring at it every night. He could almost hear her sweet voice and laughter when he looked at it. Reggie had caught him talking to it a couple of times, so he was sure his brother thought he was losing his damn mind and he was right to think it too, how could he possibly begin to try to go on with life without Makia by his side?

At least the cowardly bastard who was responsible for this tragedy was now in jail and would never see the light of day outside of a prison cell again. Rydwan said as much and that was as good as gold in Hayes' eyes.

The day they found Michael, Hayes felt like God gave him a small gift to make up for taking Makia away from him. The look of sheer terror on his face when he opened the door and saw him and Reggie standing there still brought a satisfying smile to his face. They worked him over until they both got tired and it took all the strength in Reggie's body to pull Hayes off of Michael before he killed him.

They called in an anonymous tip and left through the service entrance of the five-star hotel they found him in. He was just living it up despite the fact he had just murdered his wife! The son of bitch thought they were room service. It was well worth the five grand each he paid the five hotel employees to look the other way.

"Grandma Lo, I want you to meet Hayes. Hayes, this is our grandmother Lola or Grandma Lo as we call her." Sage made the introductions. "And this is his brother Reggie, he did his best to protect Makia from that coward," she continued and smiled as Hayes gave the white rose he was carrying to her grandmother and Reggie gave his rose to her.

Hayes smiled at the beautiful elderly woman who was a darker version of Sage and Makia. He could tell not only their good looks but also their kind hearts came from their grandmother, her sweet face said it all.

"Nice to meet you, Makia talked about you a lot, I'm so sorry for your loss," he told her shaking her hand, followed by Reggie who did the same.

"Loss? Sage, what is he talking about? Doesn't he know that—" Sage covered her grandmother's mouth and nodded to the minister, who was standing next to the urn that was positioned on a white marble pedestal.

"We are all here, you can begin," she told him with a small smile. She leaned over to Hayes, "Grandma Lo is having a really hard time letting go," she explained nervously looking over her shoulder past the minister. Hayes followed her gaze and noticed two men in suits standing off in the distance but watching them intently, one was recording them.

Feeling heated, he moved to walk towards them and Reggie stopped him. "Let it go, Bro Bro. This ain't about none of that messy shit today, it's about Makia," he stated, his hand on Hayes' shoulder.

Hayes refocused on the minister as he gave Makia's eulogy, staring at the portrait of her that was next to the urn and pedestal on a stand. She looked a little younger than she was when he met her but still so beautiful. Hayes looked up at the sky at the birds above them as once again his eyes filled with tears, how could this be real?

---

## Two months later

"Hay, Ryd's here, man," Reggie told him as he was sitting down on the patio staring off towards the trees where Makia used to draw. He looked up as his father stepped out on the patio, holding a thin white envelope.

He had taken a leave of absence from Hansen, Reggie was running the gym, he just wasn't ready to rejoin the world just yet so most of his time was spent at Paradise like he was now.

"How are you holding up, son?" Rydwan asked, handing him the envelope as he sat on the edge of the lounge Hayes was sitting on.

"I don't even know, Ryd. I'm just numb, I can't believe she's gone. He fucking killed her, man. Does it look like they are gonna convict?" He sniffed, wiping away a few wayward tears flipping the envelope over in his hands. "What's this?" he asked Rydwan opening it.

"With me working on the case, you know they will but forget that, right now I'm worried about you. Me, Reggie, and your mom decided you need a break. My treat, you fly out in the morning," Rydwan informed him in a no-nonsense way.

"Man, Ryd, I appreciate you, Pops but I'm not ready to sip Mai Tai's just yet," Hayes told him passing him back the envelope with his itinerary in it.

"Funny thing is I don't remember asking you, son. Now you can walk on that airstrip in the morning or I can knock your ass out and have Reggie carry you onto the plane, your choice," Rydwan threatened pushing the envelope back in Hayes' hands.

"Fine, Ryd, why the hell did you pick the Maldives though? There ain't shit out there?" Hayes asked, glaring at him and Reggie who was standing with his arms folded behind Rydwan.

"Because," Reggie said with a sarcastic grin. "Just go, bro and regroup. Wash your ass too," he teased, his hands fanning the air in front of him as if Hayes smelled.

---

Hayes double checked the address on the house against the address Rydwan had given him looking confused, the front door was open which was odd, because there was nothing in the description about staff at the house and it looked like people were already there. Maybe the owners double booked?

He was about to call Rydwan to ask him when Sage walked out on the balcony on the second level, spotted him and waved with a big, happy smile.

"What the fuck?" Hayes muttered waving back and stepping out of his Lyft. After grabbing his suitcase from the driver he rushed up the walkway and rang the doorbell.

Things got stranger when the not so helpful young nurse he had threatened the night Makia was attacked opened the door. Her smile was timid and a little fearful as he eyed her suspiciously.

"Hayes right?" she asked, extending her hand in his direction when he stepped inside.

"Yeah, but what are you doing here?" he asked her taking her hand suspiciously.

She frowned at him in a confused way just as Sage walked into the room.

"Allison, I will get him settled, and you're free to go for the day. I know you mentioned wanting to take Jonathan down to the beach before it rained," Sage told her, smiling at her sweetly.

What kind of twilight zone shit was this? How could Sage forget how useless the nurse was the night Makia went to the hospital and now it looked like she had hired her to take care of her grandmother or something? And why were they in the Maldives anyway?

"Thank you, Sage, and nice to see you again, Hayes," Allison said and moved towards the back of the house.

Hayes watched her retreating back with a frown before turning back to Sage. "What is she doing here? Is your grandmother okay? And why in the blue hell are you and Ms. Lola here instead of Virginia?" Hayes asked, still trying to figure out what the hell was going on and why his father sent him here. It was obvious Rydwan knew Sage and Lola would be there, as his father never did anything by accident.

"Grandma Lo is fine, she is actually down on the beach herself with a few of her friends in a dance lesson. And to answer your question, after being threatened more times than we could count by Michael's people not to testify, we sold the house and the studio and moved here. We know he will think he won but we have every intention of testifying but Virginia no longer felt like home with Ma– Never mind that, follow me," Sage said as she turned and started walking down the hall in front of them.

The walls were lined with dark wood, he noticed the 'Home' series pictures of Sage and Lola and the three of them doing what they loved most. Since he had the self portrait of Makia, they had hung her picture from her memorial service on the wall. Hayes ran a frustrated hand down his face and fell in step behind her, cussing Rydwan out the entire time in his head. Of all the people he didn't need to be around right now was Sage and Lola! It hurt too damn much!

At the end of the hall, Sage knocked softly before opening a closed door and peeking her head in. "He's here," he heard Sage say to someone before fully opening the door and stepping out of the way so he could enter the room.

He looked at Sage still frowning as he walked past her and into the room. When their eyes met, all of the breath left his body, there was no way he was seeing what he was seeing, no way in hell! He blinked and the view never changed, a very bruised but very much alive Makia sat on a bed, tears sprang from her eyes as she gave him a small lopsided and strange smile.

*"What in the entire fuck!"* he yelled looking from Makia to Sage and back again.

"Makia said you would say something along those lines. She can't speak by the way, her jaw is still wired shut for a bit longer, now calm down and have a seat, and I'll explain everything to you," Sage told him gesturing that he could move closer to Makia.

"This makes no fucking sense! I stayed in that room holding your hand until she took her last breath!" He shook his head in disbelief, praying to God he wasn't dreaming and she was actually really there all while getting heated at the same time.

"No, you stayed in the room with me until I sobbed she was gone and you helped me out of the room," Sage corrected sitting on a chair next to Makia.

"My sister the actress, I swear." Makia wrote on a wipe board shaking her head, casting a withering look at Sage.

It made Hayes smile that in spite of the situation, she was still a smart ass! God, he loved this woman and still couldn't believe she was alive! He just needed to know what the hell was going on like immediately! "Explain," he requested, sounding a lot calmer than he actually felt. His emotions were all over the place, jumping from happiness, to disbelief, to confusion, to anger and back again.

He moved closer to Makia and reached out to touch her but chickened out and let his hand drop to his side. So instead she reached out and gently pulled him down to sit next to her on the bed. The feelings and emotions that began to slam around in his body the moment she touched him had his eyes filling with happy tears.

"Well, Michael put a hit out on Makia. He really was trying to kill her that day. He was on some real 'if I can't have you, nobody will' type shit, also he wanted everything including her trust to go to him when she died. He found out about the lawsuits and divorce and needed to get rid of Makia fast because that would be the quickest way to get some money and disappear. His lawyers are just as shady as he is and figured out a way for him to take the money and run before the charges were filed.

"When she lived, it fucked up his plans and he lost his shit and hired someone to finish the job, he figured he could just play the grief-stricken husband at the horrible things someone did to his wife and when she died collect her trust and disappear. Remember at that point he didn't know about the cameras at the studio," Sage stated matter of factly, lightly touching Makia's hand. Makia had yet to take her eyes off of Hayes.

"And you know all of this how?" Hayes asked, wishing he would have thrown one more blow at Michael. He would ask for forgiveness later but he prayed Michael was being beaten every day in jail, since prisoners hate abusers.

"Your father told me. I guess as you were rushing out talking to him, he was rushing in another way talking to you and you two missed each other. At first I thought he was the security you were talking about until he introduced himself and asked where you were, then he told me everything about Michael and the hit and we needed to act fast and get Makia moved. I guess you guys had taps in the house or something? Michael was so arrogant he was talking and making arrangements out loud while he was packing to go into hiding. Like a casual conversation, talking about the price to kill his wife!" Sage shrugged and stood up again.

"So why did you let me think she was dead? I have been in a very dark place since that day, Sage." Hayes sighed, shaking his head.

"Blame your father, he was the one who arranged for Makia to 'die' and all of us to be brought here, including Allison. He said it was easier to keep an eye on her that way, because she was the nurse on duty when we moved Makia and he told me you texted him to find out more about her and her son since your PI was looking for Michael."

"But why fake her death especially after he got arrested?" Hayes wondered out loud. He was calling Rydwan and Reggie's asses as soon as he could wrap his head around all of this and the ass-chewing they were in for would make their ears bleed! In the meantime he lifted Makia's hand to his lips and kissed it softly and mouthed the words, "I missed you so much, baby girl." She touched his face in response.

"Two reasons, one, the hit was still in effect. The guys on the beach at the memorial service? They work for Michael and have been following me and Grandma Lo since the last day at the hospital. At first they pretended to be insurance adjusters with questions about Makia's life insurance policy, but when they kept asking about her autopsy even after we provided the death certificate, I called Ryd and he found out who they really were and fast tracked us out here. Second reason was because of Makia's will and power of attorney. I guess Ryd and Makia got together and drafted an ironclad new will before everything went down and in the event of her death or injury, everything came to me. The trust, the properties and everything she was to be awarded in the divorce settlement from Michael and because of the physical abuse she got it all, so when she 'died' I got it all. Guess my parents aren't that useless after all, they were the ones who insisted on that clause. Though, they never intended for it to be Makia's escape hatch but theirs. I suppose they thought when Makia said they were dead to her after the wedding she really didn't mean it so they would only have to bide their time and when they saw evidence that Michael was abusing her they would have another payday at Makia's expense. Ryd is the greatest of all time for real and found the clause, he didn't miss a damn thing in those contracts." Sage smiled over at Hayes and Makia and walked back towards the door.

Hayes shook his head in disbelief at Sage. "I thought those men from the beach were there for me the day of the memorial service, they had been sniffing around me and Reggie for a minute. When I saw them there I was about to wreck their shit until Reggie stopped me," Hayes mused still in disbelief. He knew his dad was the shit but damn, he was more calculated and detail oriented than he even realized!

"Well we can put them and all of that nasty business behind us now. Why don't you two catch up a little bit and I'll let Grandma Lo know you made it here in one piece, Hayes, she's been driving me crazy asking about you. Oh and don't be surprised at the sizable wedding gift I give you when the time comes. I hope in time you can forgive me for helping your father with all of this behind your back?" Sage asked, looking at Hayes with a sheepish smile.

"Sage, you did all of it to save your sister so I get it, I would do the same thing for Reggie if I had to and I know my Pops isn't one to take no for an answer, so yeah you're forgiven," Hayes told Sage moving his hand through Makia's curly hair, the minute his fingers came in contact with it, he gave up an immediate prayer of thanks. His baby was alive!

Hayes was still in shock and fought the urge to pull her tightly into his arms. even though she looked ten times better than the last time he saw her, she still looked fragile as hell.

"Baby girl, you have no idea how much I've missed you, I wasn't sure I even wanted to live anymore. I tried to kill Michael when I found him, Reggie had to pull me off of him," he whispered, pressing his forehead against hers, stray tears escaped his closed eyelids.

She pulled the dry erase board onto her lap and wrote "Please let that be the last time you mention that man's name to me, ever."

He kissed her on the forehead and moved her until she could rest her head in the cradle of his arm, against his shoulder. "Am I hurting you? I'm sorry if I am but I can't believe you are here, really here. By the way I never noticed you were left-handed until now," he told her, touching her anyplace he could reach that wasn't bandaged or casted.

"I'm ambidextrous and no you're not hurting me, I won't break. I need you to hold me close, I've missed you too Hayes and not seeing you all this time hurt even more than all of this ever could. When I woke up, after making sure Sage and Grandma were okay, you were the first person I asked for but they told me I couldn't reach out for obvious reasons. We had to make sure I was declared legally dead and make it believable and since Michael knew about us, we had to make you believe I was dead too. Remember when you said it's easier to tell a lie when you believe it's the truth? Besides, I was pretty messed up with no way to talk to you anyway. We were out here by the time I was coherent enough to communicate this way. And now I'm all yours, I mean if you still want me to be?"

Hayes looked from the dry erase board to her several times, her last question made him a little upset so he ignored it. "I understand, well sort of. Me, Ryd and Reggie have some talking to do. This entire time I've been asking God for one chance to see you, to apologize to you for letting this happen to you. We trusted the wrong person and you paid for it. I don't know if I will ever be able to forgive myself for that misstep," Hayes told her, looking into her still black ringed eyes. She was still the most beautiful woman he had ever seen. He reached out to touch her again to make sure she was really there, really real.

Makia shook her head in the negative and pointed to the dry erase board underlining her question. Hayes was annoyed she asked him that damn question a second time, what the hell did she expect him to say?

"If I still want you? What the hell kind of question is that, Makia? You're lucky, baby girl. If you were feeling better and I wasn't in shock, I'd spank you for asking me a question like that. Look at me, do I look like I've been okay? Baby girl, I was devastated that I lost you! Of course I still want you, look at me! I couldn't sleep, barely ate, I was talking to a painting of you in my bedroom!" he snapped looking at her like she was crazy, tears forming in his eyes as he remembered how lost he felt the minute he walked Sage out of that hospital room.

Overcome with emotion of what they both had been through in the last few months had him taking her in his arms again, holding her close until she moved in his arms to let him know it was a little too tight of an embrace.

"Sorry Makia, I mean baby girl, I mean, shit, now that Makia Hansen is dead what am I supposed to call you?" he asked her after readjusting to make sure she was comfortable again.

"Haven't got that far, what do you want to call me?"

"My wife, my soulmate, the love of my life, my baby girl, the mother of my children," he answered, taking her left hand and kissing her softly on the knuckles.

"Yeah I want to be called all of those things but that can't be my name, Hayes."

Hayes looked at her thoughtfully as he nodded and agreed with her, thinking of a name for someone as perfect as Makia was… then it hit him, "What about Angel? Angel Purcell?" he asked her kissing her lips softly, once again thanking God she was still alive.

"It's simple and pretty, but why Angel?"

"Because that is what you are to everyone you love, our guardian angel right here on Earth," he told her, wiping the tears that began to fall from her eyes.

"It's beautiful and I love it almost as much as I love you, some of my last thoughts before well you know… was how I was on short time of being able to plan my life with you."

Hayes kissed her again, and lightly touched her face, he could feel the stiff metal that held her jaw shut and traced every scratch, scar and bruise on her face, comparing to the last mental picture he kept of her and smiled. She had healed so much already.

"Damn, you still take my breath away you know that? I love you so much my Angel and since you are technically divorced *and* dead, how soon do you want to get married or do you want to live together for a while first?"

"Is tomorrow too soon? I think we waited long enough, don't you? I'm ready to live my new life as your wife."

He chuckled before kissing her again. "I tell you what, how about a week from tomorrow? I have to get my family here, you still need to meet Mom and we have to tell her she has a daughter-in-law now, since Ryd and Reggie already know. Come to think of it, where is here anyway?" he asked looking at her with a confused frown.

Makia took her left hand and gripped the dry erase marker and began to draw, it brought happy tears to his eyes. He was sure Michael thought breaking all the bones in her right hand was the final crushing and devastating blow to Makia but he failed at that too. After several minutes she finished and turned it around for him to see.

He grabbed the dry erase board and looked at her drawing, she had drawn a picture of a beach at sunset, complete with a palm tree and birds flying away in the distance, and lovers watching the sun go down, right in the middle she had written the words: Paradise, welcome home, my love.

# Chapter 9

*Present Day*

**M**akia, AKA Angel when she was in public, stood on the beach behind her and Hayes' house. The gentle sea scented breeze lifted her curly hair as she watched the sunset, a small content smile played on her face. She thanked God every day for her life, the last six months as Mrs. Angel Makia Purcell had been her dream come true. 'Dying' was the best thing to ever happen to her.

"I thought this is where I'd find you, think you're coming in anytime soon?" Hayes commented as he walked down the beach towards his beautiful wife. Seeing her so relaxed and happy always warmed his heart.

He had just finished up his bi-weekly conference call meeting to make sure all his business ventures were still under control in Virginia. Every other month he flew back to the United States to personally check on things at the company formerly known as Hansen's Holding Company, now named Purcell and Associates where he was CEO.

No one but his family knew where he lived now and he

intended to keep it that way. His number one priority in life was keeping his family safe, especially Makia, and shortly after they were married, he arranged for them and her entire family to relocate to Byron Bay, Australia. They lived four houses down from each other on the same beachfront. His heart soared with happiness as her face lit up with her now lopsided smile.

"Yeah, I was just enjoying the sunset while you finished up, Grandma Lo and Sage told me to tell you hi. Did you know your mom was flying out next week? I guess she and Grandma are going to Sydney or something for the week," Makia informed him, reaching up and draping her arms around his neck.

Hayes' mother Haleema was just as sweet and welcoming as the rest of his family and, as Makia soon found out, just as stubborn as her grandmother Lola. The family matriarchs hit it off from the moment they met and spent more time together in person and on the phone than Makia and Sage did.

"Hmm, didn't know that, and I just talked to her earlier too. I swear that woman is beginning to think she's grown or something," Hayes quipped leaning down to kiss Makia softly on the lips.

She came up on her tiptoes and grabbed the back of his head, pushing her tongue deep inside his mouth. Her tongue swirled with his before moving in and out of his mouth. A low moan vibrated deep inside Hayes' chest as he pulled her closer, his hands trailed down her body gripping her ass and grinding his growing erection against her. He felt her nipples grow hard and press against his chest as their kiss deepened. She used her left hand to take the ponytail holder off of the end of his braid and worked her way through his hair until his long dreads were loose and free, surrounding her with the lime and coconut scent of his dread spray mixed with the Blue Nile scented oil he always wore.

"Mmm, you taste good, you smell good, perhaps we should find out if you feel good too," Makia whispered looking at Hayes, her eyes sparkling with the last hints of sunlight on the beach.

Hayes sighed, pulling his head away from her, shaking his head sadly, "Baby girl as much as I love you, I'm warning you, you are going to get more than you wanted by playing with my emotions and teasing me. Do you want to sit comfortably later? You know I have the worst case of blue balls in history, six months is a long time to lay next to someone you've wanted for years and not be able to touch them." Hayes informed her, dropping his arms to his sides, and taking a step back from her.

Because Makia had very extensive healing to do, there had been a lot of kissing and heavy petting, but they had yet to consummate their marriage. Makia reached out, grabbing him by his shirt, and pulled him close to her again, pressing her lips to his before turning him loose again. "Aww poor baby, perhaps we should do something about that, especially since Dr. Armstrong gave me the green light this afternoon?" she suggested with a wicked grin, backing away from him towards the house, watching for his reaction.

A sexy grin spread across Hayes' face as her words sank in and he began to follow her. "Hold up, so you got the green light hours ago and you're just now telling me?" he asked her, his gait taking on that of a predator's.

"Well yeah, I mean you were still in your meeting when Sage and I got back from my appointment and I didn't want to disturb you so I started dinner and came out here to watch the sunset," she answered, still walking backwards. The look he was giving her had her stomach turning somersaults. He hadn't been the only one suffering, she wanted him so bad it took everything inside of her not to go into his office, close his laptop, climb in his lap, and go for the ride of her life when she got back from the doctor's office earlier.

"Didn't want to disturb me? Woman, I swear you were put on this earth to drive me completely outta my damn mind!" Hayes growled rushing forward and sweeping her up in his arms when he caught her. The savory smell of smothered chicken, rice, and sauteed squash and zucchini dominated the air when they came inside through the sliding door that led to the patio.

Hayes still held her in his arms and pressed his lips to hers before pushing his tongue as deep inside of her mouth as it would go. Makia returned his kiss, wrapping her arms around his neck as she repositioned herself in his arms.

He tore his mouth from hers and kissed her behind her ear, down her neck to her shoulder and back up again. He used his head to nudge her head back and rained kisses down on the sensitive area on her neck beneath her chin, which caused Makia to moan closing her eyes and squirming in his arms as she felt sensations of arousal begin to move through her body and congregate in her now tingling pussy.

Hayes continued his journey down the front of her body, the anticipation of finally being able to make love to the woman he loved was doing a number on his self-control.

He used his teeth to pull down the front of her sundress, exposing her breast and wasted no time, swirling his tongue around one erect nipple then the other before drawing one slowly into his mouth. One of his hands moved underneath her sundress and between her legs in one fluid motion and she felt him move her panties to the side as his finger slid slowly inside of her.

Makia's core immediately flooded with her honey, welcoming his probing finger inside of her wetness. He slid a second one inside of her, moving them both slowly in and out of her, the voice of want inside of her went from an insistent whisper to a demand of need instantly.

Hayes continued to suck on her breasts, pulling and

tugging and biting her nipples lightly as her moans began to echo throughout the room. She moved, trying to meet the thrust of his fingers while trying not to force him to drop her at the same time because she was still cradled in the crook of his arms.

Makia's entire body was awake with desire, she wanted him so bad she could taste it. Her inner walls quivered with want when all too soon, he pulled his fingers from her wet middle and sat her down on the edge of their dining room table before dropping down on his knees in front of her, licking her juices from his fingers. His hooded, lust filled eyes stared deeply into hers as he savored the taste of her.

Reaching under her dress again, he slowly slid her bikini underwear down her legs and tossed them to the side when he took them completely off. He lifted her left leg and kissed her on the inside of her ankle before biting it lightly.

Jolts of lust rushed up Makia's leg at the contact and congregated in the wet lower half of her body. A sizzling sound from the stove temporarily penetrated her sexual fog. "So I guess it's safe to say you're not hungry?" she asked softly, nodding towards the simmering pots in the kitchen.

Hayes chuckled and ran his hand up her leg, covering her entire pussy with his large hand, sliding a finger between her quivering second set of lips and flicking her clit causing her to jump. "Oh I'm fucking starving, just not for food." He came up higher on his knees and removed his hand and quickly replaced it with his warm mouth and tongue.

"Oh fuuck!" Makia moaned, throwing her head back, closing her eyes. Where the fuck had this feeling been her entire life? She had never experienced the most intimate of kisses and damn if Hayes wasn't making sure she enjoyed it.

Hayes' tongue swirled around her clit, his mouth sucking her juices as they poured from her opening. Makia arched her back and lifted her hips off of the table as new sensations shot through her moving her arousal to a new plateau. Hayes grabbed her by her hips and dragged her closer to his mouth and buried his tongue deep in her pussy.

He tongue fucked her forcefully, loving the taste of her arousal escaping her. Each time she overflowed, he licked her clean and started all over again and her walls began to vibrate around his tongue as she got closer to completion. He gently placed her hips back on the table and spread her legs as wide as they would go across the table. Her slippery wet clit pulsed and pushed up and forward, parting her pussy lips and beckoning him with need.

Hayes wasted no time moving back between her legs, licking up the sweet nectar that coated her pussy from her clit to her opening. He slurped and feasted on her offering like his favorite long awaited treat, moving his head from side to side causing her legs to begin to tremble and shake. The momentous feeling of rapture and pleasure dragged down her spine bathing her in a cold sweat as her impending orgasm moved closer to the surface.

Makia's head thrashed from side to side, she bit her bottom lip to keep from screaming at the top of her lungs. The need to arch her back and grind her pussy against Hayes' mouth as her completion closed in on her was met with his insistence to keep her spread wide open before him, refusing to allow her to move.

The first strike of her pleasure exploded within her, pulling her down deep in the dark hole of desire where Hayes' mind melting mouth was now holding her captive. Her screams of passion rang out like windchimes agitated in a hurricane as she was struck again and again by her release.

Hayes was relentless and showed no signs of stopping, in fact her orgasm had caused him to suck harder and for his tongue to dig even deeper. He was determined to suck her dry and lay his claim on her once and for all.

Makia's breath became short and choppy as her orgasm surged on, the ebb and flow of sweet ecstasy rolling through her body and causing tears to roll down her cheeks from her closed eyelids. Bathed in sweat, she began to babble incoherently as Hayes continued to eat her pussy like a starving mad man.

When the biggest wave of desire yet tumbled through her making her toes curl, and her high pitched screams reached opera soprano octaves, Makia was convinced her beloved husband had been possessed by a pussy eating demon and was about to scream as much when he finally let go of her legs and brought his head up, licking her lingering juices from his lips.

"Fuck you taste even better than I could have ever imagined, I can't wait to get more than just a sample," he said as he rose to his feet and walked over to the stove to turn off the noisy pots.

Makia looked at him in disbelief before dropping her head back on the table and closing her eyes still trying to catch her breath, he considered that just a sample? Holy fuck this man was going to kill her for real!

Their room was on the second floor of the house, with plush beige carpet and eggshell painted walls. They had many pieces of art decorating their room including copies of three of her favorite paintings on the wall, all by an artist from the States named W.A.K. 'Made for Each Other', 'Swept Away' and 'High on You' were a beautiful representation of falling in and building up true love.

Hayes led her deeper inside their room, past his walk-in closet and to their huge bathroom area. They had a jacuzzi tub set up on a platform with stairs that led to it and it was big enough for four people at least.

The shower was to the right, encased in smoky gray glass with water jets on all sides and above.

Hayes helped her up the steps to the tub and sat on the side of the tub turning on the water. Once it started flowing, he reached over grabbing a glass bottle and dropped a few drops of Rain bath oil into the water, immediately perfuming the air.

After putting the bottle back, he turned his attention back to Makia, pulling her into his arms and giving her a soft but mind-numbing kiss. His lips left hers and he trailed kisses and teasing bites down her neck, causing her middle to begin to thump and grow wet again.

Makia threw her head back and moaned when his lips skated across her shoulder and then her clavicle, her skin still sensitive from the episode on the dining room table. Just when she was hoping his kisses would go lower, he lifted his head up and stared down at her as he pulled her dress over her head.

"To be continued," he promised carefully draping her dress over his arm. He made quick work of her bra and ballet slippers and stepped down from the elevated platform and draped them over the chair in the corner of the bathroom.

Makia watched him coming back to her, his gait slow but purposeful, with a lick of his lips as he came back up the steps. His dreads framed his head giving him an almost untamed look and she loved it. He came to stand in front of her and pulled his shirt off and over his head in one fluid motion before pulling her close again.

Once again his lips captured hers in a searing kiss before he sat on the edge of the tub and pulled her in front of him. Reaching up he took both of her breasts into his anxiously waiting hands, his thumbs skated back and forth over the nipples. Makia's thighs went up in flames, the thumping in her center became a pounding.

She reached out and touched his face as he looked up at her. His eyes were low and dark and he gave her a wink before he leaned forward and wrapped his full lips around one nipple and then the other, treating each one to the swirling of his warm tongue and tug of his teeth.

Makia's eyes rolled back into her head as she felt her knees growing weak from her legs shaking with the sensations Hayes' tongue and mouth on her breast were giving her.

Sensing her difficulty trying to stay standing, Hayes pulled Makia down on his lap and grinned wickedly at her intake of breath because he sat her directly on his erection. The only thing between her wetness and his hardness was his zipper.

He went back to exploring her breasts when he felt the heat rising from the tub on his back. without missing a beat he reached behind him and turned the water off and the jacuzzi jets on. Makia repositioned herself so she was straddling his lap, gripped his shoulders and began to grind in small circles against his erection while he still focused on her breasts. Both of her nipples were hard and demanding attention which he was more than happy to give them.

Her moans became louder and more frequent and echoed around the room. Her body was still hypersensitive and tingled all over. "Damn Hayes, that feels incredible, I love how your lips feel on my body." Makia moaned feeling like she was about to explode with want as she ground harder against his erection.

Hayes could feel Makia getting wetter, her special scent of arousal rose from between her legs teasing him, causing his self-control to slip. He moved his mouth from her breast and grabbed her by the waist to keep her still while he was trying to catch his breath. When she fought to keep moving her hips, he wrapped his arm around her waist and lifted her off his lap, holding her in mid-air.

Both his second head and Makia protested immediately. "Look Makia, you have no idea how many times I fantasized about you being in this room with me like you are now but you keep that up and this will be over before we even get started." He moaned looking up at her, his arm still had her locked in place high above his lap.

"Then what are you waiting for? Let's get started." Makia

gave Hayes a mischievous wink and wiggled her way out of his arms. She stood next to him on the platform and kept her eyes on him as she ran her hands all over her body seductively before moving past him and sliding into the scented water.

Hayes watched her as she settled into the tub, moaning in pleasure as the jets massaged her tingling, aroused body. Trancelike he stood up and unfastened his pants, lowering the zipper painfully slowly. That last move of Makia's had him so hard he was seeing stars. His sexy dark eyes planted her in place with an aroused predatory stare as he came out of his pants and underwear.

Makia jumped in anticipation. Knowing she was about to finally make love to her husband for the first time had her mouth watering. Unable to move, trapped by Hayes' gaze as he stepped into the tub with her, causing the water to rise to the edge of the tub, her body was screaming for release when, without words, he grabbed her by the ankle and pulled her to him. his hungry mouth crashed down on hers so hard their teeth clashed, his hands roamed all over her body before settling on her waist where he lifted her high and dropped her down hard on his waiting erection.

Makia yelped in surprise, her eyes sprang open wide as she looked at Hayes, still kissing her like his life depended on it, as he slammed her hips up and down in his lap relentlessly, driving himself deeper and deeper each time.

"Oh my God, Hayes, damn, baby, damn." Makia moaned, moving her mouth from his. He caught her by a fistful of her hair and pulled her head to the side and bit down on her shoulder.

The emotions and desire he had for Makia tore at him to his core, demanding to be satisfied as he still controlled her rolling hips with one hand. He wanted his thrusts to continue to be directly in the center of her tight wetness, he wanted to go so deep that she never forgot he was there and finally she was completely all his.

Pulling her back even further by her hair until she arched her back, his mouth clamped down on her right breast and he began to suck aggressively. He felt her walls contract tightly around his hardness with every pull of his mouth, the hand guiding her hips moved to her shoulder as he burrowed deeper inside of her moving side to side and up and down leaving not one part of her inner being untouched.

Makia grabbed Hayes' shoulders and held on for dear life as he pounded inside of her. And all the years she thought a woman being on top gave her all the control! The lies you tell! This was the Hayes Purcell show!

Her walls trembled and throbbed around his massive intrusion, milking him for all he wanted to give her. Her body sang its song of pleasure as water splashed over the edge of the tub onto the tile floor. His deep moans as he continued to make her pussy his, shifted her arousal into overdrive.

She pulled his head away from her breast and brought his lips to hers, pushing her tongue into his warm mouth. His hand relaxed in her hair as their tongues stroked each other moving in and out of their mouths.

Moving his hands back to her hips, he shifted and turned them over in the tub so he was now on top. If she thought she felt him before, it was nothing compared to how she could feel him now. To her surprise, the water wasn't a hindrance to Hayes either, it seemed to be an aid, pushing him forward as he grabbed her by the ass and pulled her into his thrusts and went in even deeper.

"Holy shit, Hayes! How much dick do you have?" Makia moaned, pulling her lips away from his, beginning to feel his deep thrusts in her lower abdomen. Now, there was not one part of her throbbing middle that didn't know Hayes and she began to wonder how the hell she had lived her life this long without him.

Hayes slowed his thrusts and looked down at her with concern, "Are you okay? Do you need me to stop?" he asked, panting, still keeping a steady pace inside of her.

Makia grabbed him by his dreads and glared. "If you do, I might fucking kill you!" she threatened as desire began to climb higher making her crazy, she needed to come but didn't want this to end, she wanted to stay connected to Hayes this way forever.

Hayes gave her an evil grin and kissed her softly. "Then you might want to hold on, this shit is about to get real," he warned, putting her legs on his shoulders and grabbing the chrome bars on the edge of the tub on either side of her. Before her hands had closed completely around the bars next to his, Hayes surged forward with all the strength in his body, sending a wave of water out of the tub as their middles met.

"Oh my fucking God, Hayes! Yes, baby, yes, just like that!" Makia screamed out as she began to experience the second complete orgasm of her entire life. It began to climb up her spine, bathing her in chilled fire. Her body felt like she was being rained down on by electrifying rain.

Hayes brought his hips down rapidly, thrusting so deep, Makia started moving up the wall of the tub behind her. her breasts rose and fell against her chest as she bucked her hips to meet his rapid thrusts. Her eyes were open and low as she focused on him, her bottom lip caught between her teeth.

Her middle began to squeeze even harder, growing wetter and wetter. The more she squeezed, the deeper and harder he went inside of her, "Fuck, Makia, Baby, damn, how is it possible for you to feel this fucking good?" He moaned, moving her legs off his shoulders so he could kiss her again. He could feel she was about to come at any second, her vaginal walls had him in a tight grip vibrating all around him sending shock-waves up his spine.

He kissed her everywhere, bit her everywhere, she moaned and mumbled unintelligible nonsense as her orgasm hit her hard. The first wave of orgasm peaked and had Makia's back in a full arch as she dug her nails into Hayes' taut buttocks and threw her head back screaming.

"Oh shit! Oh fuck! Oh damn, Hayes, I love you, Baby! I love you, I love you! I need to feel this forever!" Makia screamed as her orgasm tugged and pulled her down deeper into sexual bliss.

Hayes kept sending his controlled thrust as deep as he could inside as Makia exploded all over his dick getting even wetter. He fought to maintain control just a little longer, giving her all the pleasure she needed, when his own impending explosion crept in and dragged him down with her.

His entire body stiffened as he felt all the blood rush to the tip of his shaft and release deep inside of her, he grabbed her to him and held her tight as her orgasm regained momentum and he continued to spill his seed deep inside of her.

"I love you, Makia! I love you so much, baby girl!" Hayes cried out crushing her against him, holding her tight. Once Hayes regained his strength he untangled his limbs from Makia's and stepped out of the tub, grabbing one of the giant bath sheets neatly folded on a wire rack next to the tub, he helped Makia to her feet and carried her to bed after wrapping her in the sheet.

He laid her down in the middle of their bed and lay down beside her, pulling her into his arms and kissing her softly on the forehead. "Get some rest, Love, we have a long night ahead of us." Hayes promised with a tired, wicked grin, kissing her lips softly.

Makia closed her eyes as happy tears ran down her face,

after everything they had been through, she and Hayes were finally, truly complete.

---

## Two weeks later

"Keep those eyes closed, we are almost there," Hayes instructed as he held her hand guiding her to their destination. Moments later he pulled out a key and walked her up to a building tucked in a corner of a quiet block with dark windows. He walked her inside and flipped on the lights. "Open them."

Makia opened her eyes and her mouth dropped open in surprise, as she looked around the two-story building, natural light poured in from above them from skylights. The main level had several staged sets with furniture, lamps, backdrops and even a space that looked like a street corner were scattered throughout the space, and a full kitchen.

She quickly moved up the wooden staircase to see the second level. Pushing the door open, her breath caught again. It was one of the most beautiful spaces she had ever seen in her life. The 'U' shaped space was bright and cheery on one side and the further Makia walked from the door, the darker the natural light became. In the midpoint were brand new easels, paints and drop cloths. At the back of the darkest end was another door that opened up to a loft complete with a full-size bed and bathroom.

Hayes' arms snaked around her waist pulled her close from behind. "I thought it was time for you and Sage to have a space of your own again," he whispered in her ear before kissing her on the cheek. "Do you like it? Do you think Sage will?" he asked, turning her around so she was facing him.

"Are you serious? She'll love it! I mean look at this place, it's amazing!" she answered, throwing her arms around his neck. "I love it, baby! Thank you so much it's perfect!"

He looked down at her, a concerned smile on his face. "I hesitated when I initially thought about buying this place, I didn't know how you would feel or even if you were ready to start painting again, after everything," he admitted kissing her softly on the lips.

"Hayes, painting is who I am, it's my coping mechanism, my solace and if you hadn't done this I was going to ask you if we could do something like this at the house. Now that I'm better, I've been getting the itch to get back to work. Besides, if I was able to create some of my best work under high stress, imagine what I can create now that I am completely happy." She grabbed the back of his head and brought his lips down to hers kissing him softly.

Hayes picked her up off her feet and held her tight. "So looking around is there anything you or Sage need that I forgot to have set up here?" he asked, pulling his lips from hers putting her back on her feet.

Makia looked around the room and even over the railing down at the main level before looking back at him thoughtfully. "You did pretty good, I'm only missing one thing up here," she informed him, still looking around the room.

He looked around too, with a frown. "Huh, me or my assistant are slipping then, I thought I covered it all but tell me what did I miss? I'll make sure I get it here as soon as possible."

Makia's face spread into a wicked grin as she moved out of the circle of Hayes' arms and grabbed his hand leading him to the loft. "I'm thinking about painting a series on mind blowing sex, and I think I need a volunteer for inspiration," she answered and pushed him down on the bed and pulled her dress over her head and off.

## One month later

The sound of female laughter that rose from the beach had Hayes looking over his shoulder curiously as he manned the grill. Instead of just his mom coming to visit, his entire family came to stay for a while. It was their last weekend before they headed back home so they were grilling and eating down on the beach. A canopy, tiki torches and a dining table and chairs were all set up not too far from where the ladies were.

Rydwan and Reggie were stretched out on the lounge chairs on the patio, sipping beers and updating Hayes on everything going on back home in the States.

He shook his head smiling as he watched Lola teaching Sage, Makia and even his mom, Haleema how to belly dance. Even at her age and after a mild stroke and lots of physical therapy, Lola was still able to move like she was twenty years old when she danced, being a dancer since she could walk and a dance instructor after she stopped dancing to raise her son, kept her in pretty good shape and young at heart. Her movements were smooth and fluid.

Again, seeing Makia so happy after so much pain and frustration with her healing made his smile even bigger. She was spending time at the new studio and even walking around most places with a sketch pad and charcoal again. She left small black fingerprints wherever she went.

She laughed and bumped into Sage as she bounced her hip to one side with one of Lola's purple scarves with bells at the end of each tassel tied around her waist. Damn, he loved her more than life itself.

"Hey, yo, Ryd, you might want to go get your wife before she breaks a hip or something, Mom is really throwing it around down there," Hayes teased, grinning over at Rydwan.

Rydwan stood and walked over to the patio railing, to see what Hayes was talking about. Haleema was swaying her hips from side to side, the bright orange scarf she had tied around her waist blew in the wind as she began to roll her belly. For a woman 56 years old she looked damn good! She glanced up at him smiling and winked before she moved back to swaying her hips. "Shit, don't know what the fuck you talking about, that's the best part of the trip out here. Lola's dance lessons have taught my baby all kinds of new tricks!" Rydwan informed his sons, nodding his head thoughtfully watching his wife move again. "Yeah she can still get it." He stated taking a swig of his beer as his sons exchanged looks of disgust.

"Pops! Come on, man! What the hell? We don't need to hear all of that!" Reggie said loudly with a frown getting up to go grab another beer. "Just ugh!"

Hayes closed the lid to the grill shaking his head, his face bunched up like he was going to be sick. "You wrong for that shit, Ryd and you know it," he told his father, grabbing his own beer and sitting down in the chair closest to the grill.

Rydwan was still at the railing laughing at his sons' embarrassment when movement on the patio of the house next door to Sage and Lola's house caught his eye. "Looks like y'all got new neighbors," he told Hayes, nodding in the direction of the woman who was standing on her patio. One hand was over her eyes shielding her line of sight from the sun to look down at the four ladies on the beach, the other resting on her hip. A man stepped out next to her and if they hadn't been on the patio, there would be no way of knowing the house was now occupied because there were no lights on inside.

Hayes jumped up from his seat looking over at the new neighbors. "Interesting, they must have just bought the place, the 'for sale' sign was still up two days ago," Hayes told Rydwan settling back in his seat drinking his beer.

"Interesting, we need to remind Makia and the rest of the family to remember to refer to her as 'Angel' anytime we are out here from now on to be on the safe side. Hayes, come here and check this out." The way Rydwan kept watching the couple, his jaw working thoughtfully, had Hayes rising back to his feet swiftly. The man had pulled out a pair of binoculars and appeared to have them focused on the dancing ladies.

"What the fuck?" Hayes snapped moving towards the stairs that led down to the beach, Reggie had just stepped back out on the patio and immediately fell in step behind Hayes and Rydwan as they walked down to the beach to their family.

"Hi, baby, did you see? I can finally do the hip thingy, the bells even ring the way they're supposed to! Watch," Makia informed him when he was close enough, happily beginning to bounce her hips from side to side to the music they were dancing to, the bells rang in time with the music too.

He stepped in front of her, putting his hand on both of her hips, stopping her from moving. His back was to the new neighbors' patio, blocking her from their view. Makia looked at him confused for a few seconds until she noticed the dark looks on all three of the men's faces.

"What's wrong?" she asked suddenly alarmed, looking from one of them to the other and back up at Hayes whose jaw was working angrily. The other three ladies picked up on the tension too and moved in closer too.

"We have new neighbors, for whatever reason they're watching you guys, y'all take the dance lessons inside while we go over and introduce ourselves, welcome them to the neighborhood," Hayes ordered, his voice was low and menacing.

"Okay but please keep it friendly, son." Haleema requested giving Hayes a stern look.

"No promises, Mom, depends on what his answer is for watching you all so closely," Hayes answered looking down at Makia who he still had by the waist thoughtfully.

Haleema and Sage grabbed the boom box, Lola's finger cymbals, and their cellphones and fell in step on either side of

Lola who was already moving towards Makia and Hayes' house.

"Baby, calm down I'm sure it's nothing, they probably just saw us dancing or even wanted a closer view of the table set up or something," Makia reasoned, reaching up to touch his face, trying to remain calm and not fear the worst possible scenario but she had never seen Hayes like this and honestly it made the hairs on the back of her neck stand on end.

"Baby girl, this is not up for discussion. I need you to go in the house until I find out what this is all about. You don't want to know what's going to happen if I have to repeat myself again," Hayes whispered in her ear, rubbing his hand on her bottom, giving her a serious look with a raised eyebrow and dropping his other hand from her waist.

Makia nodded and quickly turned to grab her water bottle and sandals to follow Sage, Lola and Haleema back up to the house, as a stinging smack on her ass from Hayes made her jump in surprise as she went.

They had recently entered into another phase of their relationship where domestic discipline had come into play. He had shown his dominant side to her several times but only with words, a stern look, or a warning from early on, when she was still married to Michael. But when they finally were together and past the trouble they survived, he brought it up and they discussed it. At first she had been nervous about it, especially after what she'd been through with Michael, but once she did some research and understood exactly what it was, she was all for it and had no problem submitting to Hayes. Hayes only had her best interest and safety in mind. He was her husband and the head of their household and she had no problem at all seeing him as such and even agreed to being 'disciplined' when she failed to submit to him. Times like now.

She tossed him an apologetic look over her shoulder as she rubbed her stinging butt cheek, rushing up to catch up with the ladies. She would never admit it to him but sometimes she stepped out of line on purpose to be disciplined because the thought of his palm smacking her on the ass to get her back in line kept her hot and bothered, and honestly made her feel even more protected and she loved knowing the lengths he was willing to go to keep her happy, even correct her when she stepped out of line.

Hayes watched her hurry up the stairs before he turned and fell in step beside Reggie and Rydwan silently as they strolled down the beach towards the neighbor's house, his jaw still working angrily. He didn't know what the fuck was up with the new neighbors and even if them using binoculars focused on his family was as innocent as Makia suggested, he refused to have anyone get that comfortable watching them.

So what that Michael was locked up in the States, they still kept an eye on his people, and after finding out there had been a break-in at Sage and Makia's studio recently, he knew someone was still out there looking for information regarding them. Luckily, he had the entire studio packed up and closed at the sisters' approval the last time he was there, so yeah, he was leaving nothing to chance.

"Can I help you?" the man with the binoculars asked coming down the patio steps to the beach when the three of them stopped on the beach in front of the patio looking up at him and the woman who was now looking down at the three of them anxiously.

"Yeah, you can tell me why you are out here watching my family," Hayes told him once he was standing in front of them, still holding the binoculars. Hayes stood with his arms folded and legs far enough apart that if he needed to move into a fight stance he could easily, he saw no point in beating around the bush.

"Oh these, I'm sorry, it's just that my wife and I just moved here after living in Egypt for the last six years and when we heard the music, it reminded us of the dancers there and we wanted to see if your family was Egyptian," the neighbor quickly explained looking nervously at Hayes, Reggie and Rydwan in turn.

Hayes exchanged pointed looks with Reggie and Rydwan, knowing the man was lying. "Interesting. Do me a favor and don't let it happen again, me and my family value our privacy, that's why we choose to live all the way out here, understand?" Hayes asked with a smile that didn't reach his eyes, "Oh, and welcome to the neighborhood," he called over his shoulder as they all turned to walk back down the beach towards their house.

"Hey Ryd," Hayes started when Rydwan raised his hand to stop him, pulling out his cell phone.

"Already on it, son, I'll have them and the sale of the house checked out and let you know what's up," Rydwan told him as he sent a message to the private investigator he kept on retainer.

"And I got you too, Bro Bro. I can hang Down Under for a bit, help keep an eye on things. Marvin can run the gym for us?" Reggie offered looking over his shoulder at the neighbor who was still on the beach watching them intently.

"Good looking out, and Reggie I would appreciate that considering how far the house is from my office and now that Mak- I mean Angel is healed up, I'm going to be working from the office more." Hayes walked up the stairs and rushed over to the grill to check on the forgotten steaks. "They just got here and I can't stand the new neighbors, guess we are just having surf tonight because the turf is now as inedible as shoe leather. Fuck!"

## *Present Day*

Makia was standing upstairs, leaning on the railing watching Sage setting up for her first full session at their new studio. a three-generation family portrait, they would start inside the studio and finish in the small courtyard outside behind the studio.

"Sissy, do you need any help? I have a few chairs up here too," Makia called down to Sage.

Sage looked up and blew a curl out of her face smiling. "The daughter who arranged this session was very detailed on how she wants this to go, I guess they only want the elders to sit, the adult kids to stand behind and on the sides of them and the kiddos on the floor on the black floor covering so I don't need more chairs, but can you come down and help me with floor covering?"

Makia dropped the paintbrush on the small table next to her blank canvas and moved downstairs to help Sage.

"So how's the painting going?" Sage asked grabbing one end of the floor covering waiting for Makia to grab the other end to spread it correctly.

Makia sighed and shrugged, "It's going okay, it's just that…" She started then trailed off as she spread her side of the covering on the floor in the circle of lights in front of the upholstered chairs she was using for the photo shoot. Sage had been busy with shoots since they officially opened the studio, her new freelance and portrait work with the beautiful beaches and Australian wilderness as backdrops was getting so much attention on her website that she was already booked with sessions for the next three months.

To be safe, when she had sessions, Makia made it a point to stay out of sight. "It's just that what? What's going on, Sissy, I've been up there and not one painting or sketch is finished and that's not like you," Sage stated knowingly, stepping back to make sure the setup looked right.

"I know this is going to sound stupid but do you remember the painting of Hayes I was working on that, well that was destroyed? I feel like I need to finish it before I can move on to something else and the problem is both the sketch and the canvas were ripped to shreds," Makia admitted, sitting down in one of the chairs in the circle of light. Sage flipped on the portrait lights and grabbed her camera, messing with her lens, Makia sat up straight knowing Sage was using her black shirt for balance.

"Girl is that all? I took a picture of both at the old studio, I'll email it to you when I finish this." Sage smiled bringing her camera up to her eye. "Smile pretty, Angel Purcell." Sage teased taking her picture several times.

---

Makia stepped out of the sea onto the beach in her dark purple two-piece bathing suit, the minute her feet hit the sand she felt Hayes' eyes on her. His arm was draped over his eyes shielding him from the sun above the lounge chair he was stretched out on.

Just seeing him made her stomach and pussy jump with excitement, she couldn't get enough of him. She still marveled that it took 24 years to understand what the big deal with sex was really about. if she could, she would spend every waking moment making love to her sexy ass husband.

Makia walked towards him, drops of water rolled down her body as she moved closer to him. Her hair was down, wet, curly and wild, an innocent smile spread across her face when she reached him and sat down next to him on the lounger.

"Are you done for the day or are you coming back in for a

while?" Makia asked a little out of breath, grabbing the towel off of the lounge meant for her to dry her dripping hair.

Hayes didn't answer, instead he stayed in the same position, watched her pat her hair and then her smooth, soft skin dry, lazily running his fingers up and down her spine. How much he loved Makia was almost scary, she occupied his every thought from the time he woke up until the time he went to bed, she had become his everything.

"Hello? You in there, Hayes?" Makia sang waving her hand in front of his face smiling. Sometimes the way he looked at her made her wonder what was actually going on in his head.

He wrapped his arm around her waist and pulled her until she was leaning on top of him. "You are so beautiful, I love you so much Makia, my Angel," he whispered, reaching out touching her face and then her hair.

"I love you too, Hayes and thank you, so I'm taking it that you are done swimming for the day?" she asked leaning in to kiss him softly.

He wrapped both of his arms around her and moved her until she was lying completely on top of him, his tongue pushed its way into her mouth as their kiss intensified. His hands moved down her body, cupping and massaging her buttocks as he pushed his tongue deeper into her mouth.

Her hands moved to the back of his head and set his dreads free, it tripped him out how obsessed with his dreads she seemed to be. If they were in mixed company and his hair was up, he would catch her staring at his hair biting the inside of her cheek thoughtfully, he was sure she was thinking of how soon they would be alone so she could take it down.

"No more swimming, Love. I have a better idea., I guarantee you will still work up a sweat," he whispered against her ear before biting her ear lobe and sitting up with her still in his lap.

"Hmm sounds intriguing, but I have to take a shower to

wash the salt water off first, that and the sun will kill my hair otherwise, so whatever wicked thoughts you have rolling through that sexy head of yours are going to have to wait, besides don't we have to meet with Ryd today?" Makia asked, dropping her arms over his shoulder before leaning forward to drop soft kisses on the side of his neck down to his shoulder before climbing out of his lap and to her feet.

He moaned in frustration and stood up to follow her inside the house. "For the record I was talking about the sauna but I see where your mind is now," he said, his eyes glued to her ass, Makia was fucking perfect but her ass kept him weak, perfectly round with that perfect bounce when she walked.

Hayes tried to instruct his body to behave, but the memory of her warm soft lips had him at full salute by the time they stepped inside the house. He reached for her and pulled her against him wrapping his arms around her from behind grinding his front against her round backside.

"Do you have any idea how sexy you look right now? All wet and wild?" he whispered moving her from side to side in his embrace moving as if he was moving her to music only he could hear.

A small moan left Makia's lips as she arched her back and ground against him until his erection grew more and the tip of the head of his dick peeked out of the top of his swim trunks. She turned in Hayes' arm and started kissing him softly on his chest, her lips and tongue dragged across his nipples until they morphed into hard black pebbles before her eyes.

Hayes closed his eyes and put his hands behind his back, to keep from touching her and allow her better access to his chest. She raised her head smiling up at him with a devious smile before continuing her journey down his body. He stared down at her curiously, she had never been this bold before and she had him wondering what she was up to.

Hayes knew she had very limited sexual experience as a

matter of fact he was the third man she had ever been with in her life and there was no way in hell she was about to do what it looked like she was about to do! She ran her tongue around his belly button, pushing her tongue inside a few times before kissing him even lower before pausing.

Hayes fought harder to keep his hands behind his back, he was so hard that the entire head and a few inches of his length had busted free from the constraints of his trunks. All he wanted to do was bend her over one of the dining room chairs and bury himself deep inside her wet warmth but he ignored his urges and let her play.

"I thought you were worried about your hair," Hayes reminded her looking down at her, his self-control slipping.

Makia sat back staring at his erection then up at him before getting back up on her feet. "You know you're totally right, thanks for reminding me, guess we can pick this up later? What time do we need to meet with Ryd?" she asked moving towards the stairs and their bathroom to shower and wash her hair.

"What the fuck?" His hormones and common sense screamed at him in his head. The want Hayes felt for Makia at that moment was clawing at him. He wanted to grab her and coax her to continue what she started, why the hell did he even open his fucking mouth?

"Ryd is calling at six our time, he said Michael's trial is about to start so he needs to go over some things with us," Hayes choked out, not even bothering to conceal his peeking head as he watched her moving up the stairs.

"Cool, so how much time do we have before he calls? I don't have my watch on," Makia said pausing at the top of the stairs, looking over at him, her glance lingering on his erection as she licked her lips.

"Like I said he's calling at six so that leaves you plenty of time to wash your hair and get cleaned up," he answered through clenched teeth, purposely moving his trunks all the way down past his erection before tucking it all back into his trunks, giving Makia a full view of his suffering. "And for the record, you are really asking for it, Makia."

"Good to know, in that case how much time do we have to get a little dirty?" Makia asked, pulling her top off and tossing it down to him.

Makia continued to walk down the hall towards their bathroom, peeling off her wet swim shorts as she went. She could hear him on the stairs and picked up the pace to the bathroom.

Once inside she quickly stepped inside the dark glass shower and turned on the top and side shower heads and stood under the sprays closing her eyes and throwing her head back wetting her hair rinsing the salt water out of it.

A distinct snap caused her to open her eyes, Hayes stood in front of her holding a bottle of shampoo, he was naked and his erection jutted straight out from his tangle of dark pubic hairs in her direction.

"Turn around," he ordered, his voice was low and husky causing vibrations to start moving through her as it echoed in the shower.

Makia turned around to face the shower wall and moaned out loud when one of his hands moved around her body cupping her breast while the other squeezed shampoo in her hair. He set the bottle on the shelf to her right and moved in closer behind her, his hand slid down her body and spread her second set of lips before flicking his finger across her clit, causing her opening to contract and grow wet. She braced her hands on the shower wall for more stability but he removed his hand and got busy washing her hair.

A frustrated moan left her lips as the fire he started began to burn, "Now you know that's not right, Hayes," she fussed pressing her thighs together tight while he washed her hair.

After massaging her scalp for several minutes, he leaned down and kissed her on the side of her neck. "Turn around, time to rinse," he said in the same husky voice, the minute she turned around and tipped her head back to rinse out the shampoo, he grabbed her around the waist to hold her steady and his mouth clamped down on one of her breasts. She stopped rinsing her hair and moved her hand to touch him when he stopped, looked at her shaking his head in negative, popping her soundly on her ass causing a quick intake of breath on her part.

"Don't worry about what I'm doing, rinse the shampoo out of your hair, Makia," he ordered biting the underside of one of her breasts before moving lower.

Makia closed her eyes and went back to rinsing her hair as his tongue moved around her stomach. His lips felt like the most intimate whisper as they drifted across her sensitive skin.

She moaned, softly at first then louder as he moved lower, he leaned down and tongued her belly button until she could barely stand, he kept her safe in his tight grip around her waist. Makia's wetness poured down her thighs, her clit jumped in anticipation, that stinging smack had her hormones singing.

Hayes' head dipped lower and he kissed her on top of her mound of short pubic hair. She didn't like Brazilian waxes but refused to have a dark forest between her legs like she did after being bedridden either, so a trim to keep it short was more her speed.

He used his free hand to spread her pussy lips and blow on her clit. Makia threw her head back in the spray of the shower beginning to lose her mind because of his lips. Hayes moved slowly back up her body and gave her a devious smile. "Conditioner, turn around."

Makia looked at him and whined, stomping her feet, glaring up at him. Another stinging smack on her ass had her biting her bottom lip as she turned her back to him. "You are not playing fair, Hayes," she pouted, leaning her head back against his chest while he poured leave-in conditioner on her head.

"Patience, love, I want your attention focused one-hundred-percent on me when we cross that bridge. Consider it payback for downstairs, your teasing ass should be grateful I don't have you pinned against this shower wall getting rocked instead of helping you wash your hair," he growled, pulling her head back by her hair so he could kiss her.

His words and the picture they painted were making her clit and opening quiver and pulse like there was no tomorrow, she needed Hayes in whatever way he was willing to give himself to her and she needed him now! He turned her hair loose and reached behind her turning the water off.

He grabbed her by the hand and wrapped her head in a towel and body in a bath sheet before leading her to their massive bed. It was bigger than a king but smaller than a double king-sized bed.

He sat down on the bed and removed the bath sheet, and proceeded to rub her down with shea butter he kept on his bedside table. His hands moved from her shoulders and down her arms, massaging the moisturizer into her hands and fingertips. Even him performing this simple task had Makia's senses singing, she wanted him so bad it hurt, not having him moving inside of her at that very moment was painful!

Hayes turned her around and moved his oiled hands down her shoulders, down her back to her buttocks, paying special attention to each cheek before he placed a soft kiss on her back directly above them. The move caused Makia to curl her toes and turn to face him, the entrance to her most precious treasure was right in his face.

"Girl, keep playing with me and see what happens, I'm trying to be a gentleman here," Hayes warned her, rubbing more shea butter between his hands before he reached up running his oiled hands around each breast, down her stomach and each leg.

His hand circled her ankle before moving back up her legs and between her legs, his thumb quickly swiped her clit causing her to bite down hard on her bottom lip.

Okay enough of this shit! He wanted to play, they were going to play. She didn't know a lot but she knew enough of what got Hayes to melt and purr in her hand.

"My turn." She pushed him back and grabbed some shea butter rubbing it between her hands to melt it, she got on her knees and started at his feet, rubbing shea butter on his already baby soft smooth skin.

Moving up she paid special attention to his calves and knees, when she got to his thighs she spread them and oiled the outside first, then moved her hands higher and ran her oiled fingers through his pubic hairs and even moisturized his balls.

He arched his back, his butt cheeks clenched tight as she moved on to his shaft, she came up higher on her knees and trailed her tongue slowly up his shaft to the head. Hayes' arms shot out and he clutched the sheets tightly in his fist as Makia slowly lowered her mouth on the head of his dick.

She sucked tentatively at first and increased the suction when Hayes' low, long moan of surrender had her pussy singing. Makia relaxed her throat and mouth and swallowed more of his length. Hayes began to make hissing noises as she sucked him and swirled her tongue around the head before taking him deeper into her mouth.

She bobbed her head up and down faster and faster, loving how his velvety smoothness tasted in her mouth, the way he jerked and moved beneath her as she gave him pleasure.

"Makia, baby, damn, for someone who has never done this before you got skills, girl." Hayes moaned slowly, moving his hips upward to go deeper in her mouth, while taking a hold of the back of her head and guiding it downward beginning to fuck her mouth.

He waited for her to pull back or pause because it was too much but to his surprise she adjusted her body and kept going, swallowing more of him. He could even feel her tongue flicking out to touch his scrotum!

Makia moved her head up and down, pausing to suck in the head of his dick before swallowing him whole again. Hayes began to moan and move beneath her, louder than before, his sounds of surrender, being the driving force behind her momentum. She began to taste something salty at the opening of his tip and licked his hole curiously to taste more.

"Holy shit!" Hayes shouted and pulled her off of his dick. Makia was about to mess around and have him coming down her fucking throat and he wasn't sure if she was ready for all of that.

"Oh, no, Hayes, did I do something wrong? Are you okay?" Makia asked sitting back on her feet still kneeling between his legs looking alarmed.

"No, no, no, baby you were doing everything right. My God, girl, you are amazing and a fucking fast learner. I stopped you because I was about to come and I wasn't sure you wanted me to," he explained trying to catch his breath, his hand was idly stroking his erection.

Makia moved his hand away and stroked him herself. "I want you to," she murmured before taking him into her mouth again, ready to drive him crazy to completion.

Hayes lay back and grabbed the back of her head and pumped in and out of her warm suctioning mouth, within minutes his impending orgasm ricocheted up his back and centered in his scrotum until his balls tucked tightly against his body and it shot forward up his shaft and into Makia's waiting mouth.

"Holy fucking shit! Holy fucking shit! Damn, baby damn!"

Hayes cried out as Makia continued to suck his dick, she swallowed every drop like it was her favorite ice cream, he jerked and moved his hips even faster until he emptied his entire load into her mouth. When he was finally spent he let her head go and dropped his arm heavily back on the bed with his eyes closed.

Makia moved from between his legs and grabbed the unopened bottle of water on his bedside table drinking it all as she watched his dick twitch and his chest rise and fall. She used to be the one who said she would never suck a dick but seeing how much Hayes loved it, she was all in!

Hayes' eyes finally opened, darting back and forth looking for her before propping himself up on his elbows to find her standing on the side of the bed, watching him.

"So, um, did I do pretty good for my first time?" Makia asked him shyly.

Hayes chuckled and pulled her down so she was lying on top of him. "Shit, girl, for your first time you did fucking amazing!" Hayes told her bringing his lips to hers, kissing her softly and freeing her hair from the bath towel. His hands moved freely through her hair and down her back until he was gripping her ass and grinding against her soaking wet mound.

Makia pushed her tongue in his mouth and took notice of the fact he was already hard again beneath her, she moved her legs so she was straddling him and sat up, his erection was spreading her second set of lips apart, the pressure of him pressing against her soaking wetness had her feeling like climbing walls.

When he didn't immediately lift her up and let her slide down his pole, she lifted off his lap to do it herself. The head of his dick had just touched her opening when Hayes' arms wrapped around her waist lifting her off his piece and repositioned her on his face.

Makia immediately came up on her knees in alarm, afraid

Hayes wouldn't be able to breathe, his arms locked around her thighs and spread them farther apart until Makia had no choice but to lean forward and brace herself on the headboard in front of her and settle her lady bits directly on Hayes' mouth. Hayes brought his head forward and ran his tongue up her slit and kissed both of her lower lips in turn.

Makia closed her eyes, dropped her head forward, her hands balled against the headboard. "Shit, Hayes," she moaned, she thought his lips were magical before but damn in this position, he was fucking Houdini!

Hayes' warm mouth sucked the juices of her arousal from her slit, her opening even her pubic hairs causing new sensations to course through her body, hot, sharp waves of passion rolled through her as his tongue dove deep inside her treasure. He buried his face deeper between her legs and ran his tongue around her clit before sucking on it slowly. Makia closed her eyes tighter and let out a high-pitched moan.

"Baby damn! This feels so fucking good! Please, please, please don't ever stop!" Makia cried out, finally allowing her body to fully relax against his mouth.

It must have been what he was waiting for because he gripped her thighs tighter and began to eat her out with gusto. His mouth and tongue were tasting and sampling her pussy like it was his last meal.

Makia began to move her hips, grinding against his tongue as he pulled more and more of her nectar from her center. All too soon she felt the waves of orgasm tearing through her limbs and gathered at the meeting place between her legs, she fought against her body's need of completion, never wanting this to end, for this feeling to go away.

Makia even tried to move so Hayes' mouth had to pause but no such luck, her fight to get away gave him renewed determination to drive her over the edge.

"Oh Hayes, no, baby, no! Please not yet, fuck I can't hold it back fuuck!" Makia whimpered as her rain came down, Hayes' mouth was perfectly positioned to drink every drop. Makia's body shivered and shook as Hayes coaxed her orgasm to its end with his masterful mouth.

When her tremors were reduced to small, sporadic vibrations he pulled her from her perch and rolled over so she was underneath him and slowly entered her. Her eyes popped open in surprise for a brief second before closing again as Hayes rocked her body toward bliss once again, damn she loved her some him!

## Chapter 10

"So I received the defendant witness list and that slimy son of a bitch is calling your entire family to testify Makia, your parents included. Basically he's pleading temporary insanity saying he found out you were having an affair and snapped. Seeing the answer to the charges he faces which his attorney has filed, he is basically planning on dragging you and your character through the mud as a defense. You and I have talked about this possibility when you were in the Maldives and what needs to be done Makia," Rydwan stated that night on their Facetime call.

Makia sighed and ran her hand down her face, knowing what he was referring to, she had hoped it wouldn't come to this, that she could continue to live her life in peace far away from Michael and all of that bullshit. "I remember and you're sure there isn't another way, Ryd? I mean I thought with all the charges against him this case would be just another nail in his coffin easily and like you said in the Maldives, he is relentless and can't stand losing, so if I do, won't this start all of that mess all over again? Besides, he has no proof that I had an affair because there is none. Hayes and I didn't start seeing each other until he came to the Maldives," Makia said, biting the inside of her cheek nervously at the mere thought of what Rydwan was telling her.

Hayes looked from Rydwan on the monitor to Makia with a confused look of concern. "Okay are you two going to tell me what the hell you're talking about or continue to talk in code?" he asked snappishly.

Makia sighed and sat back in her chair, shaking her head sadly. "We are talking about me going back to Virginia to testify against Michael," she told him, looking down at her hands fighting back tears of frustration.

"What? Why the fuck would that even be an option? He tried to kill her, Ryd and when he failed he tried to have her killed! Now you want to put her back in the crosshairs of whoever he hired last time? Hell no! She ain't going back to Virginia not now or ever so we need to rethink the strategy or something," Hayes fussed standing up from his chair and beginning to pace.

"Hayes, son, I hear what you're saying but I need you to hear what I'm saying as well, he's pled out of all of his other charges so right now without the attempted murder and conspiracy to commit murder charges he will be out with time served in less than eight years in club Fed, even with the sexual harassment charge from his former assistant. We want his ass under the jail and with a conviction of continued domestic abuse and attempted murder of Makia we will have just that," Rydwan calmly explained, as Hayes continued to pace back and force, agitated.

"Fuck that! I refuse to let my wife be used as a pawn or bait in that crazy muthafucka's last power trip, find another way, Ryd! Otherwise what was the point in moving her out of the fucking country? They think she's dead, let it stay that way!" Hayes snapped and slammed his body down hard as he dropped down in his leather office chair.

"Baby, calm down, I always knew this was a possibility and as much as I don't want to go back, for this to truly be over it looks like I have to. If Michael gets out of prison, he and his slimy ass lawyers are going to do everything in their power to figure out exactly where I am, where we all are and the nightmare starts over again," Makia reasoned rubbing the back of Hayes' neck to calm him down.

"Why would he when he thinks you're dead?" Hayes asked with a deadpan smirk.

"Because he knows she isn't, Hayes. Michael's lawyers are not stupid and neither is he. There is no record of Makia's death filed anywhere. I used it as a stall tactic and made sure that was the consensus until I could make the moves to get her and the family out of harm's way. If you recall even after her 'death', I still moved forward with the divorce for that very reason. When the dust settled I wanted to make sure Makia and all she was due was free and clear from Hansen," Rydwan explained patiently, Makia saw him tossing a stress ball from hand to hand.

"So everyone was privy to the fact she was alive besides me? Well what in the actual fuck? And hold up, Sage said everything was transferred to her because of Makia's will, how was she awarded everything without a death certificate?" Hayes asked, sounding calmer but still looking annoyed.

"Son, I'm hurt. You underestimate your old man; you know how I do. Sage was Makia's power of attorney until she married you and at the time Makia was not in any shape to make decisions on her own behalf so as power of attorney, I ensured everything was transferred to her until Makia was fit to govern her own affairs again."

Hayes ran his hand down his face shaking his head, "You the man, Ryd, that's what's up but back to the elephant in the room, you went to great lengths to help her disappear; is her suddenly reappearing the smartest move, Pops?" he asked, taking Makia's hand and kissing it.

"Unfortunately, it's our only move if we want to take down Hansen once and for all. Besides my associates will be driving home the fact that after the attack, Makia was not only afraid for her life but also the lives of her family, so much so that they went into hiding. Like you, my first priority is keeping her, Sage and Lola safe. I will get to arranging the security detail as soon as we hang up. If Makia agrees to doing this, you have to trust me, son, I would rather die than have something happen to them," Rydwan stated, looking stern and serious at Hayes.

"Fuck! I don't like this but I guess we have no choice, so if Makia's okay with it so am I, but I'm telling you both if that bastard comes for me or mine nothing will stop me from killing his ass this time," Hayes promised kissing Makia's hand again.

"Okay that being said, Makia, it's up to you, are you ready to return from the dead so to speak?" Rydwan asked, giving his daughter-in-law a kind and patient glance.

Makia sighed, her stomach cramped with anxiety at the thought of seeing Michael again, then she looked at the scars from the surgeries on her right hand and saw red. He tried to take everything she loved away from her including her talent. She endured over two years of hell at his hand not to mention countless hours of healing, therapy both physical and mental after the attack, she still woke up in cold sweats from nightmares from time to time.

Yeah, it was time she showed him how miserably he failed to break her, how despite his best efforts she was better now having gone through all she'd endured than she ever was before but most of all she wanted to show him how the tables had turned and now the outcome of his life rested in her hands. She planned on making him suffer, just like he took away her freedom, she would take away his, for good. "I'm ready, Ryd, let's gut punch that ass!" Makia said, mimicking

Rydwan's action of a gut punch. Making Rydwan and Hayes chuckle immediately.

"Perfect, as I said before I will get on the security detail as soon as we hang up, round the clock 24-hours a day for all three of you, anything else?" Rydwan asked sitting up leaning forward on his desk.

"Yeah, did you come up with anything on the neighbors yet?" Hayes asked and smiled up at Makia as she stood up to walk over to the bar and pour him a drink.

"Naw, nothing yet. Found out the house was bought by a corporation not an individual so Charles is digging deeper, looking into the board of directors and shareholders for the corporation. As soon as he has that info I'll hit you up. He is also partnering with someone local to you to cover more ground faster."

Hayes thought about what he said carefully, the uneasy feeling about their new neighbor intensifying, he didn't know what it was but his gut was telling him they were not to be trusted.

"Cool, just let me know what you find out," Hayes said, accepting the drink from Makia, kissing her hand again. "Thank you, love."

Makia leaned down and kissed him on the lips. "Anytime love, you looked like you could use one."

"Oh God here y'all go with all of that newlywed shit! Anything else before it gets R-rated up in this piece?" Rydwan snapped, smiling and shaking his head.

"Whatever Pops, I remember the last time you and Moms was here, I'm still trying to get y'all's loud ass moaning and groaning out of my head! And yeah one last thing is there anything and I mean anything else you two are keeping from me?" Hayes asked pulling Makia on his lap just to spite Rydwan.

Rydwan cleared his throat and looked at Makia with a small smirk, "Anything else you need to tell him, Makia?"

Makia narrowed her eyes at the screen and draped an arm over Hayes' shoulder. "Nope, nothing that I can think of at the moment." She leaned forward and kissed Hayes again.

Hayes looked from Makia to Rydwan and back again before nodding his head, "Okay, now remember you both said that so if I have to dig in y'all's asses later you know why," he warned taking a sip of the drink she made him.

"Noted and I'll be in touch with the trial dates and when I need you all out here. Anything else?" Rydwan said, setting his stress ball down on his desk.

"Nah we good, Pops, keep us posted and good looking out as always," Hayes answered reaching over and wiggling the mouse on his computer to wake up the cursor to log out of their video chat.

"Cool, and no problem, talk to you both soon. Makia, don't waste one-minute worrying about any of this, just like Hayes, I will wreck him and his lawyers and anybody else for that matter who tries to fuck with my family especially my daughter-in-law," Rydwan promised his serious face spreading into a bright smile.

"Thanks, Ryd and talk to you soon," Makia said, waving to the monitor and resting her head on Hayes' shoulder.

"All right then, Pops," Hayes said before clicking end on the chat and repositioning Makia in his lap until she was straddling him.

"You good?" he asked pulling her ponytail holder out of her hair, which fell forward and framed his face. He pushed it back with his hands and leaned forward to kiss her softly.

"I'll be all right, I just don't like the idea of having to see him again, but this is what I have to do," she answered when he pulled his lips from hers.

"Yeah but you don't have to face him alone, I'll be right

there with you, we all will. In the meantime, anything I can do to make you feel better so you're not stressing all night?" he asked lightly touching her face, she could feel his dick beginning to stir beneath her.

"You already know what I need," she said smiling and brought her lips back down on his and pushed her tongue inside of his mouth.

Hayes moaned low and grabbed a handful of her hair as he deepened their kiss, Makia pulled her arms out of the straps of her sundress and pushed it down to her waist. Hayes let go of her hair long enough to lift her off of his lap to free himself and settle her on top of his erection, she moved her hips in a circular motion taking him deep inside of her pussy slowly inch by wonderful inch.

"Close your eyes, love, push all of those thoughts out of your mind and enjoy the ride," he whispered as he grabbed her hair bringing her mouth to his again and began to move.

---

"Wow, what a beautiful painting." A female voice dropped out of the serene sound of the beach as Makia painted a few evenings later and had her looking over her shoulder.

Their impending trip danced in the back of her mind trying to worm its way to the forefront, so she felt painting on the beach would quiet her anxious thoughts while Hayes was at work.

The older woman that lived next door to Sage and her Grandma Lola was standing behind her, admiring her painting of Rydwan, Haleema, Reggie and Hayes. Hayes recently asked her to paint a portrait of them for their anniversary, he wanted it to have the same family feeling as her collage style painting of her, Sage and Lola.

Even though she had plenty of time to finish it, she started on it because she knew once she got back to Virginia, she wouldn't be in the mindset to work on it then.

"Oh, thank you. It's not finished by any means but I like how it's turning out. I'm so sorry I haven't had the chance to introduce myself to you or your husband, my name is Angel. Angel Purcell," Makia answered smiling over at the woman, extending her hand to shake.

"Nice to meet you, Angel, my name is Ella. Now which twin are you? Our immediate next-door neighbor or the wife of the handsome young man who never seems to smile?" she asked moving closer to the painting.

Her description of Hayes made Makia chuckle, she could see how the woman came to that conclusion. He wasn't too trusting of her and her husband after the binocular incident when they first moved in.

"The wife of the guy who doesn't seem to smile and Sage is just my sister not my twin but we get that a lot," Makia told her going back to the painting.

"So the beautiful older woman who dances, is that your grandmother?" she asked moving even closer to Makia's painting.

"Yes, her name is Lola," Makia answered, beginning to paint again.

"The man in the painting here, he was here the first day we arrived too wasn't he? I remember him and your husband were with this young man, your in-laws, I believe?" she asked, still studying the painting pointing at her pencil drawing of Reggie, leaning on his pride and joy Regina before smiling over at Makia again.

Makia looked over and noticed Ella's smile didn't reach her eyes, her eyes looked almost annoyed. Her stance and posture were really tense and all wrong for their conversation.

"Wow, you have really been studying us, haven't you? Why so many questions now, Ella? If you wanted to know more about us you could have just come to introduce yourself sooner."

"True, but you know how it is moving to a new home, you are never truly finished unpacking for at least a year right? Speaking of unpacking, some of the artwork I recently purchased just arrived from Italy, would you like to come inside and take a look? I would love to get the opinion of such a talented young lady like you," she offered, flashing her toothy yet not really sincere smile again.

Makia suddenly felt anxious, the way she always did when Michael was in the house but too quiet. She hadn't felt that way in a long time and immediately wanted it to go away. "Uh, no thanks I really need to get back to work but thanks for the offer, it was nice meeting you." Makia forced a smile in Ella's direction over her shoulder before going back to painting, praying her subtle change in body language was enough of a hint for Ella to move back down the beach towards her own house.

"Well, some other time then? I figured with your obvious love for art, you would be interested in seeing some of my more priceless works of art," Ella said, still standing in place. "I'm curious, you don't have an accent, is it safe to say you're from the U.S.? May I ask where you're from originally?"

Makia was treated to that same fake ass smile, yeah she needed this lady to move the hell on already! "Considering we just met, I don't feel comfortable divulging that information," Makia stated honestly facing Ella again.

"Oh come now dear, you would think you were hiding from someone or something. I'm just trying to be neighborly and make conversation that's all." Ella simpered moving even closer to Makia.

Makia took a step back and dropped her paintbrush in the rinse water, making sure she would be able to get in a fight stance if she needed to. She was back to practicing her kickboxing two to three times a week, but hadn't even had thoughts of putting hands on anyone until today. Yeah, something was most definitely up with this woman.

"Look, as I said before, I don't feel comfortable discussing that or any other personal things about myself or my family with a complete stranger, neighbor or not. I don't know you and I hope you can understand that. Now if you will excuse me I would like to get back to my work," Makia stated with a tight smile.

Much to her relief she spotted Reggie and Sage walking their way up the beach. Reggie split his time between both houses, he and Sage had grown very close over the past few months, it seemed they had the same taste in women and were constantly hanging out together, being each other's wingman.

"I understand, Angel and my apologies for overstepping and making you uncomfortable." Ella folded her arms and pulled her sweater tight around her body as Reggie and Sage stepped up.

"Hey Sissy, who's your friend?" Sage asked moving past Ella and hugging Makia, something they always did when they saw each other since Makia's assault.

"Oh this is Ella our new neighbor, she came down to introduce herself, she's been unpacking and hasn't had a chance to get around to meeting all of us," Makia informed her and Reggie, giving Sage a pointed look when she let her go. "Ella, my sister Sage and brother-in-law Reggie," Makia said introducing the three of them.

"Lucky you, Ella, you get to kill several birds with one stone." Sage turned and reached to shake Ella's hand who now seemed nervous since she and Reggie arrived.

"Yes, lucky indeed but I can see you need to get back to work, Angel, so we'll talk again soon. Nice to meet you both," she said before smiling at all three of them weakly and rushing up the beach towards her house.

"What the hell was that all about?" Reggie asked, frowning at Ella's retreating back.

Makia shrugged and pulled her paintbrush out of the water. "I have no freaking idea, Reg, but something is off about her. She was perfectly content to stand here interrogating me until you two showed up."

Sage looked down the beach at her too. "Yeah, I ain't feeling her at all, she's got some bad juju or something going on, like she's hiding something and I'm still not over that whole binocular thing."

Reggie pulled out his phone and turned to walk towards Makia and Hayes' house. "Yeah well, I don't trust her or her Peeping Tom ass husband, Imma call Ryd to see if he's found out any more about those two."

Makia sighed watching him go. "Girl, the sooner this trial is over and behind us the better, otherwise I think all the Purcell men are going to lose all of their damn minds!" she said going back to painting.

Sage chuckled and looked down the beach at Ella who was now standing on her patio watching them. "Yeah well, let me tell you until it's all over, I sleep a little better at night knowing they are always on alert. after what he did to you we have no idea what other kind of crazy Michael Hansen is capable of," she said lifting her camera zooming in on Ella's face making sure the picture she snapped of her when she was standing in front of her was clear enough to give to Rydwan. The Purcell men were not the only ones on high alert.

―――――

"Ay yo 'Kia you got a package, looks like a new canvas," Reggie informed her after knocking and walking into her part of the studio.

Reggie had pretty much taken on his previous role as bodyguard again, he came and acted as security at the studio when they worked there, it made the sisters feel a little more at ease knowing there was always someone looking out for them.

Makia knew Reggie didn't really mind doing it because of all the good-looking women constantly coming in and out for photo shoots who were bold as hell and kept flirting with him and giving him their phone numbers.

"Thanks, Reg but I didn't order a new canvas. Hayes stocked this place with every shape and size canvas I could dream of wanting for at least a year," Makia said, walking over to him taking the package, smelling oil paint immediately. "I think it's a painting actually," she told him with a confused frown.

She set it on an easel and cut away the paper and twine and what she saw had her shaking immediately, her breath picked up to panicked pants and she felt lightheaded as she looked at her own work. Her final project when she was studying for her degree in Italy. A self-portrait with a full view of the inside of her head, dark colors on one side showed herself in chains, tattered clothes in a dark room, tears in her eyes. The prison she was in, being forced into marrying Michael. The dark colors blended into lighter colors on the other side of her head where she painted herself smiling, broken chains dangled from her wrists as she ran into Sage and Lola's outstretched arms, they were high above the burning world below them, standing in the clouds. She entitled it 'My Hell for Their Heaven'.

Reggie was instantly at her side, "What? What is it, you painted this right?" he asked, suddenly alarmed, he knew her style and signature enough to know this was hers but didn't understand why she was so upset about it.

Makia nodded as fear rose up and began to strangle her, she tried to speak, to tell him what this meant but she couldn't seem to push the words past her lips. Tears sprang to her eyes remembering the pain and frustration of that time of her life. She never knew what happened to it other than it was purchased for one of the highest prices at the auction showcasing student's work. So the fact that someone sent it here, to Australia, under the name Angel Purcell meant whoever bought it knew who she was and where she was.

"Sage! Yo come up here right quick!" Reggie called out beginning to panic because Makia was still silent. Tears poured from her eyes as she hyperventilated.

Sage came through the door at the top of the stairs all smiles until she saw Makia in full panic, rushing forward. Sage grabbed her in her arms, looking over her shoulder at Reggie and mouthed, "What happened?" He pointed at the painting and shrugged before moving to pick up all the discarded paper from the painting.

"Hold up! Isn't this that painting I told you was beautiful but I hated because of what it represented? Where the fuck did this come from and who the fuck sent it here?" Sage asked looking down at Makia before the papers in Reggie's hand. "Check the packaging, Reggie, see if there is a card, postmark, return address or anything," Sage ordered walking with her arm around Makia to take her downstairs.

"Sissy, did you ever know who bought it, I mean did they ever give you the person's name or anything?" Sage asked her a few minutes later, sitting across from her at their small round table in the kitchen of the studio.

Makia was slowly sipping a cup of lavender and chamomile tea, her breathing was finally returning to normal. She could hear Reggie speaking in tense hushed tones from upstairs, she assumed he was probably on the phone with Hayes or Rydwan or both.

"Sage, I told you then, I had no idea who bought that damn painting but the fact that it was sent here, addressed to

'Angel Purcell' is not a coincidence!" Makia said her breath catching again as Reggie walked into the kitchen.

"Hayes and the private investigator Ryd hired to help him over here are on their way over. I told him I didn't know what the hell was actually going on but after I found the card tucked in the corner of the frame, I thought they needed to come down here," Reggie informed them sitting down on one of the high stools at the kitchen island handing the card he found Makia.

She read it and burst into tears again. Sage snatched the card from her hands and read it herself, "Free at last, but for how long? See you soon!"

---

"So it's obvious whoever sent this shit knows exactly where Makia is and probably has for a while. They sent it as a warning," Rydwan said, stating the obvious. "I submitted my revised witness list to the courts, the day after we spoke."

Hayes, Makia, Sage, Lola and Reggie were all crowded in Hayes' home office for a conference call with Rydwan that evening. After Makia filled him in on why that particular painting made her so emotional and she hadn't seen it since it had been sold, the private investigator took the painting and all of the packaging it came in to check it for fingerprints.

Hayes asked everyone to meet at their house to discuss things with Rydwan, it was obvious someone knew where they were and wanted to play games especially with Makia so they needed to figure out who it was and what their next steps to ensure their safety needed to be.

"It's Michael, it's got to be him, his sick ass is probably the one who bought that painting to begin with but how did he figure out where I am?" Makia said pacing back and forth behind the rest of them that were all seated, with her arms folded biting her thumbnail.

"Makia no doubt he has something to do with this but, knowing he is still locked up, we need to know who is out here doing his bidding. That person or persons are my biggest concern right now, it's obvious Michael is using them to shake you up and maybe even scare you into not testifying."

Makia scoffed and rolled her eyes heavenward. "Well, at first, they almost did just that until I realized either way I am going to face Michael again and I might as well do it on my terms not his, the bastard," she snapped still pacing, Hayes stood up and pulled her into his arms to calm her down again.

"Exactly that, baby. Michael Hansen wields no power here or anywhere for that matter unless we give it to him. He knows you're coming for his head and is getting nervous." He kissed her on her forehead and led her back to his chair, pulling her on his lap.

"I bet money it's Ella and Mr. Binoculars' ass! Do we know anything else about them, Ryd?" Sage asked, taking a sip of her iced tea in front of her.

"Not on them in particular, just that the company listed on the deed to the house is a fake name for a company named Zills and Bindi in Dubai. I am in the process of finding out the ownership now," Rydwan informed them looking through some papers on his desk.

Lola took in a sharp intake of breath and began humming low, rocking back and forth shaking her head slowly. Sage reached over and took one hand, Makia sat up on Hayes' lap and grabbed the other, "Grandma Lo, what's up?" Sage asked, looking confused.

"My Lord in Heaven, why have I been cursed with such a child?" Lola mumbled, shaking her head with a sigh.

"What child, Lola?" Hayes asked, touching Lola's shoulder reassuringly.

Before she could even compose herself to answer, the doorbell rang. Reggie swore under his breath as he rushed out of the office to answer it, he came back in a few minutes later with a familiar couple in tow.

"Oh *hell no*! What the fuck are you doing here?" Sage snapped at the couple, surging to her feet angrily. Makia looked from her parents to Sage, a look of disbelief and shock on her face.

## Chapter 11

Evelyn Sallow looked her eldest daughter up and down with disdain before focusing on Makia who was still sitting on Hayes lap in the circle of his arms, a look of shock on her face. Jason Sallow took one look at Hayes and the hostile glare on his and Reggie's faces and stepped back into the hallway.

"Why are you here?" Makia asked evenly, her rage for her parents was barely controlled and rolled off of her in waves.

"Makia! Do you know what you've put us through? We have been looking everywhere for you! Do you have any idea what kind of mess you've caused since you decided to up and disappear from Virginia?" her mother demanded moving further inside the room.

"Decided to leave? Wow, just wow, there is so much I could say about that but none of that matters right now, I just want to know why the hell you and your spineless husband are here in my house!" Makia surged off of Hayes' lap and was in her mother's face with a quickness.

"Because we came to get you and take you back before you

cause any more damage than you already have. You need to stop all of this foolishness and come back to Virginia and help your husband, that's why!" Evelyn snapped glaring at Makia.

"Evelyn, I don't know what the hell that man told you but I don't need to go to Virginia to help my husband because my husband is right here! Michael and I are divorced!" Makia snapped at the poor excuse of a woman she once called her mother, pointing at Hayes. Her father was still standing in the hallway shifting from side to side nervously.

"Oh my God, Makia, you can't be serious! Please tell me you didn't marry this man! Do you realize what will happen to us if Michael Hansen finds out about this? That his suspicions about your infidelity were true? It makes our agreement with him null and void! You and your selfishness have ruined us!" Evelyn shouted in Makia's face accusingly, her entire face trembled in frustration.

"Evelyn, shut the hell up! It's your fault you and my spineless son are in the situation you're in, not Makia's! It's not her fault you made a deal with the damn devil! Ever since Jason let you talk him into pushing me out of my own company, you have been sucking up the money like the bloodthirsty leech you have always been. I warned him about you but he didn't listen. The only good to ever come from you two are my granddaughters! It sickens me to know I invested and saved to secure a future for this family and you two have liquidated and sold off every piece of it bit by bit and now you have the nerve to stalk into this child's house trying to make demands and guilt her into feeling sorry for you after you sold her to the highest and most violent bidder? Did you even bat an eyelash when you found out what he did to her, Evelyn?

"You have the nerve to say she chose to up and leave Virginia, she wasn't even conscious! He tried to kill her and we moved her to keep her safe! And for what, Evelyn? Money and his ego. Lastly, I will not have you or the barracuda of a bully

Michael Hansen tossing accusations Makia's way because I know for a fact Makia was never unfaithful to that bastard because *I* raised her better than that!" Lola had risen to her feet and moved Makia out of the way standing toe to toe with Evelyn.

"Oh please! It doesn't matter if that's true or not, it's what is perceived, how it looks! Michael is willing to give her another chance to save face and her reputation and if she had half a gnat's brain she would take it!" Evelyn spat at Lola.

"Evelyn, you have about five seconds to get your greedy ass the hell out of this house, and take that coward I used to call my son and the people you have squatting in that house down the beach with you! Speaking of which, be prepared to provide all the paperwork to that house because it looks like Zills and Bindi belongs to me and my grandbabies!

"God, just when I convinced myself you couldn't sink any lower or be any dumber, you send your former maid and butler here to spy on us? You should have seen their faces when she opened that door and saw me standing there! I knew I saw those two before, scurrying down the beach at night peeking in windows and digging in trash!" Lola snapped, shaking her head.

"I always wondered if that stroke affected your brain more than you were letting on and obviously it has, you transferred everything but your house and that damn studio to Jason, remember? We own that piece of crap company, not you sweetie," Evelyn simpered tossing Lola a smug look.

"Interesting, I guess it's safe to say me and your daughters aren't the only ones Jason was willing to double cross for the love of money. He sold my dance and supply company back to me a year ago," Lola informed her chuckling mirthlessly as Evelyn whipped her head back and forth, glaring at Lola then Jason several times sputtering angrily.

"That's right you're playing by my rules, Evelyn and it

looks like you're out of moves and money, so before I have you and the jellyfish in the hallway arrested for theft and fraud, I strongly suggest you get your ass out of this house and off this island and back to your miserable lives in Virginia," Lola hissed looking deadly.

"And Evelyn, pass on a message for me please? Tell that coward of an *ex*-husband of mine, that I, Mrs. Angel Makia Purcell am coming back to Virginia. I'm coming back on my own terms and I am coming with one sole purpose, I'm coming for his fucking head!"

---

## 12 weeks later

Makia slowly paced back and forth with her arms folded outside of Courtroom J. She worried a piece of loose skin on her thumb as she waited for the doors of the courtroom to open, to finally know the verdict and her ex-husband's fate.

For five long days, she had been grilled and questioned until her nerves were grated raw. Pictures of her beaten and bruised after Michael's last brutal attack and those taken by Hayes before it were paraded around the courtroom for the world and the jurors to see.

She shed tears for the woman in those pictures, she was a stranger to Makia now and it made her blood boil to think with all the evidence of what he'd done to her, people still sided with him and blamed her for all of it.

Michael's lawyers tried to pick apart every bit of her testimony and as predicted accused her of having an affair, an affair with Reggie not Hayes! When they dropped their 'bombshell' Makia actually choked on her own saliva to swallow her laughter.

"Hey, baby girl, I need you to eat something. Regardless of

what's going on, I won't allow you to forget to take care of yourself," Hayes informed her, handing her half of a turkey sandwich, keeping the other half for himself.

"Thank you, baby." Makia stopped pacing long enough to grab the sandwich and take a bite before she started pacing again.

Hayes sat down on the bench next to the courtroom and reached out grabbing her hand and making her sit down next to him. "Stop worrying, you came here, you told the truth, we all did, that's all we can do. It's out of our hands now," Hayes told her, kissing her softly on the cheek.

"I know but I keep wondering if the truth is enough." Makia sighed nervously, laying her head on Hayes' shoulder.

"Remember the first day you came to 'Paradise' and Reggie and me both told you to relax because you were with the good guys?" he asked her kissing the inside of her wrist giving her chills.

Makia smiled and nodded, remembering moaning over chicken wraps and sitting in the circle of trees and her charcoal drawing of Sage. "Yes, I remember, I hadn't felt that hopeful in a long time at that point," she answered.

"The same still applies, baby girl, you're with the good guys now and none of us will ever let anything happen to you or anyone in our family for that matter. I said it once and I will say it again fuck Michael Hansen, don't you waste even another moment of energy worrying about his ass," Hayes ordered giving her a stern look before kissing her again. "Now finish your sandwich, they should be coming to get us in a few." He put his arm around her and pulled her close. She rested her head on his chest and quietly finished her food. The sound of a courtroom door opening caused Makia to open her eyes a while later, she had nodded off, still wrapped in Hayes' arms.

"The jury is back," Rydwan told them looking somber and serious.

"Four hours and twenty-three minutes, you called it, Ryd,," Hayes said checking his watch standing to his feet and helping Makia to hers. Rydwan had predicted a verdict in five hours or less.

"Yeah, well when you've been doing this for as long as I have, you get to know how certain cases play out. He held the door open for Makia and fell in step beside her, Hayes followed behind them and sat down in the first row behind their table as Rydwan pulled out her chair for her to sit.

Makia felt his eyes on her the minute she entered the court-room, she turned and glared in his direction the minute she was settled in her chair. He tried to play on the jury's sympathy by coming to court looking worse for wear, his normally neatly trimmed and edged up fade was overgrown and worn in a barely shaped afro, he had dark circles under his eyes and the expensive suit he wore was at least two sizes too big to give the appearance he lost weight. Even with something as serious as this he was still trying to game the system.

Michael had tried even harder to intimidate her in any way possible leading up to the trial, phone calls, letters, even a shady looking man with prison tattoos on his face hanging around her grandmother's house, like they would have been stupid enough to stay there while they were in town! All attempts backfired and were reported to the judge immediately. Still just to be on the safe side, Sage and Lola went back home to Australia with Reggie as soon as they testified against him.

She kept eye contact with him as they were instructed to rise for the judge. A smug smile spread across her face as she saw him stand and swallow nervously as the jury foreman cleared her throat to read the verdict. Her face spread in a full smile when he was found guilty on all of the charges against him and sentenced to seventeen years in prison for the solicita-tion of murder charge alone.

The moment she would remember forever was when she

hugged her father-in-law and rushed into her husband's waiting arms. The look of shock and disbelief on Michael's face was priceless as he was handcuffed and realized that everything that once belonged to him was hers now, including his freedom.

## Epilogue

*Two Years Later*

An excited baby squeal had Makia looking up from the canvas in front of her, a bright smile lit up her face instantly seeing her 18-month-old son running from Sage and Lola's house in her direction on fat toddler legs.

As usual, he was barefoot so she was not surprised to see Hayes hot on his trail with tiny sandals dangling from his fingers trying to catch him.

"Mommy! Mommy!" he squealed as he reached her and practically climbed up her legs to get away from Hayes and the dreaded shoes.

"Hey, Mr. Man, did you have fun at Grandma and Auntie's house?" she asked, hugging him close and kissing him repeatedly on his fat cheeks.

He was a perfect blend of her and Hayes, he had his daddy's intense dark eyes and skin tone with her crazy curly hair and eyelashes. She could tell he would be tall like Hayes and Reggie. Reggie was already saying he was going to be a heartbreaker like him.

They had decided to wait to have kids but like every other part of their life what they had planned and what actually was were two different things. Shortly after they returned home from Virginia, Makia found out she was pregnant. When they told the family, Rydwan informed them he already knew, said her face gave it away on the video chat when he told her he needed her to come to Virginia to testify.

Regardless, everyone was beyond happy and Hayes Jr. was born into and surrounded by love. He spent his time between the three houses his family owned. Rydwan and Haleema called the house next to Sage and Lola's home now that they had moved there too.

Sage was seriously dating again, her new girlfriend was a ballet dancer who was 100% her equal in every way. She spent a lot of her time with them, teaching them to dance on the beach with Lola. Makia was sure they were going to announce their engagement any day now if they didn't just sneak off and get married first.

Hayes and Reggie sold the gym and opened one closer to home, three blocks over from Makia and Sage's studio. Now that Michael had been convicted and she no longer had a reason to hide, Makia was teaching art classes at the studio as well as doing commissioned work again.

Reggie was still Reggie, the only true love in his life was his car, Regina. He told Makia he was just going to enjoy being young and single until someone had his nose open the way she had Hayes.

All in all, Makia's life was as perfect as it could be at the moment, she even forgave her parents for their part in her nightmare of a marriage to Michael and even thanked them for bringing him into her life at all. She came to realize if she had never met Michael that horrible night at her parents' house, she would have never met Hayes and even more than that, being in such a terrible marriage before helped her appreciate the wonderful marriage she had now.

"You know he can open Sage and Lola's screen door now? I turned around to get this boy's shoes and he was out! He's fast as hell too!" Hayes told her, his hands on his hips trying to catch his breath. "And look here, Wild Man, it's about to be me and you if you don't put these shoes on." Hayes grabbed one of his son's feet and immediately Hayes Jr started kicking.

"No! No shoes!" he fussed, trying to get his feet away from his Daddy's hands. Makia held her hand out for his sandals and kneeled down sitting her son down next to her, without a word between them Hayes Jr held up one foot then the other as she put on his sandals.

"How the hell do you do that? This boy fights me like I'm about to kill him about his damn shoes," Hayes asked, shaking his head.

"He just likes when I do it," she answered with a shrug, laughing at the feigned hurt look on Hayes' face. Hayes Jr spotted Rydwan walking down the beach towards them and took off running in the direction, screeching happily at the top of his lungs

Hayes kept his eyes on him until Rydwan swept his grandson into his arms before he looked back at Makia, her bright calm smile always caused his heart to contract with love. He reached out and pulled her close against him before pressing his lips to hers. "Like my son, I like it when you do it too, only I'm not talking about helping me with my sandals," he whispered, pressing his lips against her ear before kissing her again pulling her even closer.

Makia pulled her lips away from his with a wicked grin. "Oh really? Exactly which 'it' are you referring to?" she asked lightly biting his bottom lip.

"All of them. Yo, Ryd, the wild man is crashing with you

and Moms tonight, cool?" Hayes called over his shoulder, grabbing Makia by the hand hurrying towards their house.

"Cool," Rydwan called back and began to chase Hayes Jr. down the beach towards his house.

Hayes swept Makia up in his arms when they stepped inside the house, kissing her as he walked through the house to their bedroom. He gently laid her in the center of their bed kissing her gently as he removed her clothes. "Damn, how the hell did I get so lucky?" he asked looking down at her as he pulled off his own clothes and joined her on the bed.

"Funny, I was just about to ask you the same thing," she answered, closing her eyes as he entered her.

Makia's love for her family was her greatest strength and her biggest weakness. Once where there was nothing but pain, there was now true love and the loyalty of a family she knew would walk to the ends of the earth to make her happy just as she would always do for them.

The End

# Joy Bussu

Blessings! I am 48-year-old Joy Bussu. Eighteen years married, mother of four, grandmother of one. I was born in Wichita Falls, Texas, but raised in Denver, Colorado, where I currently reside with my beautiful family.

I have always had a love for the written word. I devoured books from the time I could string sentences together and I have always loved to write. Once I gave birth to my youngest child and only daughter, I was finally ready to attempt to write my first book. It took me over ten years to complete it.

Holding the first copy of my self-published book was the opening of the flood gate I never even realized I was holding back. Writing is my passion and my life and it is my pleasure and deepest honor to be able to share it with the world. My dream is to touch as many as humanly possible with my work.

Visit my webpage

Don't miss these exciting titles by Joy Bussu and Blushing Books!
Whispers
Makia's Bodyguard

*Anthologies*
12 Naughty Days of Christmas 2020

# Blushing Books

Blushing Books is one of the oldest eBook publishers on the web. We've been running websites that publish spanking and BDSM related romance and erotica since 1999, and we have been selling eBooks since 2003. We hope you'll check out our hundreds of offerings at http://www.blushingbooks.com.

## Blushing Books Newsletter

Please join the Blushing Books newsletter
to receive updates & special promotional offers.
You can also join by using your mobile phone:
Just text **BLUSHING** to 22828.